# Celebrity Spin Doctor

## Celia Mulder

Cats in Libraries Press

# DEDICATION

To Grandma Celia, the National Enquirer, and Queen B, all of whom inspired this book in one way or another.

# CONTENTS

# CHAPTER ONE

"No, I don't think having a baby with my ex is a *viable solution*. What the fuck does that even mean?" screamed Christy-Anne from the other end of the phone. "Whatever. This isn't *Celebrity Goss Weekly*, this is my fucking life. What the hell are you thinking?"

"Christy-Anne, calm down—"

"You're fired, L. For real this time." Christy-Anne hung up.

Lucille shrugged and turned on her tablet. It was the fourth time she'd been fired since this morning.

"One, two, three, four, five," she counted as she checked her email.

The phone rang again. She waited until the last ring, then answered with cool professionalism. "Hello, Lucille Anton, publicist, speak—"

"Don't give me that shit, L. You know it's Christy-Anne."

"Christy-Anne, what a surprise. I take it I'm no longer fired?" Lucille settled into her high-back leather desk chair, wondering how far they'd get this time.

"Yeah, well...I want to hear your fucked-up plan."

"I know that having a fake baby with Ryan sounds crazy—"

Christy-Anne snorted.

"But here are the facts of the matter. You are a hot, sexy, international pop star, a role model to teen girls everywhere, the cause of wet dreams for men from thirteen to sixty-five. You are the face of teenage romance." She spoke with the care of someone facing a rabid dog that would jump up and bite her face off at any moment.

"I know, cuz like, I'm me. Duh."

"Right, so, given all that, how do you think it'll sound if your fans find out you'd been having an affair with a married man half the time you were with Ryan? And that you weren't the only one said married man was screwing? So far no one has linked you to Marcus, but you know how fast rumors turn into allegations. Do you really want to be a part of Marcus's downward spiral?"

*Damn, I'm good.*

"No." Christy-Anne's voice was petulant rather than enraged.

"If people think you're having Ryan's baby after a passionate reunion weekend, which supposedly happened at the same time that fan ran into you and Marcus, it'll distract from the affair. Plus, if they think Ryan abandoned you once he found out about the baby, you instantly become the tragic, jilted heroine. Just think of how many songs you can write about being broken-hearted and pregnant."

"You think?"

"Absolutely. Audiences love a reunion of their 'it' couple as much as they love a dramatic break-up. You'll be giving them both."

There was a long pause accompanied by the sound of Christy-Anne chewing. "But won't people notice I'm not pregnant? You know, when I like don't have a baby?"

Lucille smirked. "Don't worry. You don't have to keep it up for long. Just until your charity concert next month when you'll announce it was a false positive and you have been too devastated to talk about it."

"Charity concert?"

"Yes, the free concert you're doing to raise money for cancer research."

"I'm not getting paid for that?"

Lucille decided not to explain what charity meant. "After that, no one will even remember about that photo of you and Marcus at the music awards."

Another long pause. More chewing. "Fine. But I'd like to know why you can't tell me about these things sooner. Maybe I'd wanna know I'm knocked up before I read it on the Internet."

"Christy-Anne, you know why I can't. If you knew about the story first, we'd have lost that crucial, honest reaction of heartfelt denial when the press confronted you."

"Yeah, whatever."

The door to the study, her temporary office, opened, and James L'Andre strolled in, one eyebrow raised. Lucille glared at him. He pointed to his diamond-studded watch and glared back at her.

*Right, the damn movie launch.* Just another tedious party full of horrible people that started in less than an hour. If anyone other than Raphael had requested she meet a potential client at a film launch after-party, she'd have laughed. But this was Raphael, her oldest, most consistent client, and he said the meeting would be worth her while. Her interest was piqued. She mouthed "five minutes" to

James and shooed him out the door. He went, rolling his eyes, his silk thong in a bunch.

"Wait..." Christy-Anne called Lucille back to the conversation at hand. "Isn't the asshole your client too?"

"Leave Ryan to me. You just focus on getting lots of rest and throwing in some morning sickness here and there. You're pregnant now."

Christy-Anne swore loudly. "You're fucking lucky I love you, L, or we'd be over."

"I know."

Lucille hung up and shook her head. For someone who'd changed her name to Christy-Anne and sang pop love songs to the tweens of America, she had a pretty dirty mouth. It would have made Lucille laugh if she weren't the one in charge of the smut-talking singer's image.

Now that the love-child story had been picked up by *Everyday Fame*, called in by her paparazzi contacts, it wouldn't be long before it caught on. Soon the Internet would be plastered with Christy-Anne's face, the headlines screaming absurd speculations about Ryan's reaction, whether he really was the baby daddy, and how long it'd take her to lose the pregnancy weight. The media was reliably thorough in its celebrity trashing.

Lucille smiled as she packed up her office for the day. Any moment, Ryan would call. She'd traced him to Miami, where he was no doubt on a beach with a few blondes and too many beers. With luck, he'd still be there, obstinately drunk, when the press caught up with him. Ryan would be ridiculed for abandoning Christy-Anne in her time of need. He'd have to make a huge romantic gesture to get back into the public's favor, big enough to leave the scandal with Marcus well and truly forgotten.

James was waiting in the downstairs parlor of the Victorian nightmare she was forced to call home. The parlor had been updated as a den for a family of six or more, with TV hookups, a huge sectional, and built-in bookshelves of dark wood. Though she wouldn't be there long, it was long enough that those had to go. Now the room was a pale mint, just a shade off from white, with a vanity and salon chair where the bookshelves would have been. She'd gotten rid of the couch and had no need for a TV. The only movies she watched sat on the table by her bed, and all but one were collecting dust. Thus, the former family room now contained a few exorbitantly expensive sculptures, original works of postmodern art, and little else.

"I didn't think you were coming back," Lucille said as she sat down in the salon chair facing the vanity. At the last black tie event, James had had the audacity to put her in a peach dress. She'd caused a minor scene when she was close to being on the best-dressed list for her daring gown. The grief she'd given James over it should have made the grown man weep.

James laughed as he whisked a black cover over her casual jeans and silk blouse. "What can I say? I'm a masochistic bastard. Besides, what other stylist would be willing to make last-minute house calls?"

"With the amount I pay you? Just about anyone."

Lucille's phone rang. James ran a brush through her dark hair. "If you answer that, you'll be late."

Lucille rolled her eyes. "I'm already going to be late. That's the point."

"I mean late late. Like, e v e r y - one-turns-and-stares-at-you-as-you-walk- through-the-door late. Now, am I doing a full updo or leaving it down?" His comb scraped along her scalp as he teased out the snarls.

Lucille bit back a wince. James may have been rough, but he was a genius with hair. "Down. Since

I am neither getting married nor going to the prom, I will, as always, be wearing my hair down."

James sighed. He was also a master of the updo. His creations had graced the pages of every fashion magazine and runway in town. However, they tended to stand out and, as she constantly reminded him, the last thing Lucille wanted to do was be memorable.

Her phone rang again. It was Ryan. "I've got to take this," Lucille said, trying to pull out of his grasp.

He released her head, scowling. "Fine. But this time it won't be my fault they notice you walking in. You asked me for a rush job, not a miracle."

Lucille smiled sarcastically and walked down the hall to the horrendous vintage kitchen.

James yelled after her. "If you mess up that hair, it doesn't matter how much you pay me. I'll still kill you."

Leaning against the butcher block countertop, she answered, "Lucille Anton."

"Anton, it's Ryan," bellowed the voice on the other end. There was a lot of noise in the background, shouting and cheering and the cries of seagulls. He was at a beach then, not, as often was the case, a strip club. Once he'd called from a Miami spring break luau he was crashing, shouting over the partying coeds.

"Ryan, darling, it's been ages. How are you?"

"Fucked. Everything is really fucked."

*Say what you will about them, Lucille thought, but there was never a couple more perfect for each other than Christy-Anne and Ryan.* Thank God they hadn't figured that out yet. It kept her in a job.

"Oh, I'm sorry to hear that. Is this about the baby?"

"Don't fuck with me, Anton. You know it is. What the hell?"

"So you saw that article about Christy-Anne?" Lucille kept her tone sweet and soothing. She wanted Ryan to know she was on his side, but she couldn't resist messing with him just a little.

" Obviously I saw the fucking article. Not right away, of course. I thought it was more bullshit about her. Then some chick says she won't fuck me because I abandoned my goddamn baby! I thought she meant Monica and I told her that bitch lied—"

Lucille wanted to bang her head on the counter to block out this conversation. She didn't, in case it messed up her hair. For a man who couldn't weigh more than a hundred and twenty pounds, James could be terrifying.

When Ryan took a breath, she jumped in. "I know. It was wrong of me not to tell you first, Ryan. But think about it this way—how did you learn about the article?"

"Um, a reporter showed up at my yacht earlier. He asked me what my reaction was, and when I told him to fuck off, he made me read it."

"And what was your reaction?"

"I was pissed."

"And surprised?"

"No shit."

"Exactly. If you'd already known about the baby, you wouldn't be surprised when the reporter confronted you, right? This way, the press believes that you honestly didn't know anything about it. What'd you say to the reporter?" Lucille checked her nails. She needed a manicure but didn't have the time. They'd have to do.

"I said it wasn't fucking true, of course. I didn't even know she was pregnant and I'd never run off on my kid. Again."

"I know that, Ryan. But see, since you didn't know about the baby, you were able to deny it honestly instead of only pretending to be upset."

There was a pause. In the background some people cheered and called to Ryan.

"I'm on the phone, dumbass," he shouted. To her he said, "So if I had known about the baby, then I would have sounded fake."

"Precisely."

"Okay, I get it, right, but like, you're supposed to be my fucking publicist too, Anton. This makes me look like shit."

Maybe James would do a manicure. Her chipped nails looked awful. Anyone she spoke to would see the missing polish. "I'm on your side, Ryan. I always have been. Yes, the article didn't help your image, but that's where part two comes in. You're going to Christy-Anne's—"

"No fucking way."

Lucille sighed, more to her nails than him. "Hear me out. You go to Christy-Anne's house, apologize, and—"

Ryan snorted.

"—say that you want to be there for her while she's pregnant and you're going to be the best dad ever to this little baby. Christy-Anne will have no idea you're coming. You'll look like the saintly boyfriend who doesn't run from his mistakes, and she'll look like the conniving hussy who got pregnant just to get back at you."

She could hear Ryan thinking about it, his living brain cells desperately trying to function despite years of abuse.

"That's fucking brilliant, Anton," he said finally.

"I know. Be at the airport by five a.m. tomorrow. Your plane leaves at six." Ryan started to protest. "If you get there early enough, you may be able to catch Christy-Anne pre-makeup."

Ryan laughed. It wasn't a nice laugh.

Years ago, Lucille would have thought it cruel to sic Ryan on his ex so early in the morning. Now she didn't care. Was it cruel she'd booked his six a.m. flight an hour ago, before knowing he'd agree to go? No, that was called being prepared. Perhaps it was mean not to tell Ryan the baby was fake, but after three years of working with him, she knew his acting was terrible at best.

Lucille ended the call with one last reminder. "Don't forget to play up the redemption and forgiveness. The story will leak by noon tomorrow and be everywhere by Monday. Monday afternoon you'll once more be America's favorite boy-band superstar."

She hung up and rolled her neck back and forth, trying to stretch the elusive kinks.

"James," she said as she returned to her bored stylist. "How fast can you do a mani?"

James looked up from his phone and let out a long, slow, intentional sigh.

Lucille smiled and sat back down in the salon chair. The party would be starting about now. By the time the polish dried and her hair was finished, not to mention she'd fitted herself into her Spanx and a tight dress, she'd be beyond fashionably late and bordering on rude. She'd sneak in the side door. Her mysterious potential client was the only one expecting her and, while she was dying to find out who Raphael would risk his reputation for, she wasn't about to show her curiosity by arriving on time.

# Chapter Two

*There is nothing worse than an actor turned screenwriter.* Brett scowled at the melting ice cubes in his empty glass. *Correction: there is nothing worse than a party for a stupidly brilliant actor who turns out to be a stupidly brilliant director AND screenwriter.*

Brett ordered a refill. It was an open bar, after all.

The Bonne burst with A-listers, B-listers, and some C-listers who hadn't been caught by the bouncers yet. They clumped together like teenagers at a school dance, too self-involved and cliquey to interact in other social spheres. In the corner lurked the directors, none of them on speaking terms with each other or their former actors. The suits—agents, publicists, and producers—networked the hell out of everyone. They popped from group to group, using casual acquaintances as currency for entry and leaving a cloud of business cards in their wake.

In the midst of it all, beside the vaguely ostentatious ice sculpture of himself and surrounded by a steady stream of jealous well-wishers, lounged the host and honored guest, Raphael DeCarte. To live in LA, hell, to live in the world, and not recognize Raphael DeCarte, was a social faux pas on par with going barefoot in a public restroom. There hadn't been an Academy Award-winning film in the past ten years that hadn't had Raphael's hand in it as actor or producer. Studios had been on his case for longer than that to get him to write and direct. The one that had finally succeeded was media conglomerate Stanton Enterprises, and the patriarch himself, business mogul Lou Stanton, stood beside Don Raphael, accepting his congratulations with a triumphant smirk.

Stanton Enterprises. Not strictly a production studio—that would be too simple for Lou Stanton. A dangerous business man, he had a hand in every type of business imaginable. It was even rumored the man owned the Internet. While that rumor had yet to be confirmed, it was common knowledge Stanton Enterprises owned half the hotels in LA, including the one they were in. To have Lou Stanton attend in person meant that Raphael DeCarte had achieved a level of stardom few could attain. Hell, Brett was related to the guy and that hadn't stopped Stanton from firing him.

Brett threw back his whiskey and was about to order another when a flash of dark hair turned his head. He squinted, feeling the eighth drink in the back of his eyeballs. There, across the room, climbing the white staircase to the second-floor balcony, was the reason he was here.

Michel Polce, multi-millionaire, Oscar winner, media sensation, and fashion icon whose Italian love ballad CD had been the first foreign language album to hit number one on the American pop charts. He had the look of a romance hero: muscular, angular, and handsome. He was an enigma, a mystery, a shadowed Lothario, entrancing and utterly unattainable.

He also happened to be Brett's former best friend and, for the night, Brett's date. Or, rather, Brett was his date. All Brett knew was that, after not speaking to him for over two years, Michel had sent him an invite to the party with a note saying, "This is a matter of life or death."

The writer in Brett, long dormant, had stirred at the challenge. He'd dusted off his tux, combed his hair, and shown up—only to discover Michel was nowhere to be found. Now that he'd spotted the bastard, there was no way Brett was letting him get away.

He abandoned his glass on the bar, wobbling as he slid off his stool. He shoved his way through a crowd of B-listers, ignoring their protests, never taking his eyes off Michel.

Michel disappeared.

Brett blustered with open-mouthed indignation. He made a dash for the stairs, busting through a group of anorexic teen actresses like they were dry twigs. On the far side of the teenagers, he ran headlong into a pair of ultra-fake, permanently perky boobs.

"Brett Jacobs," said a shrill, surprised voice from behind the boobs.

He wilted.

His chase had been impeded by a tall, thin woman in a plunging mauve dress, her equally mauve lips scowling at the sight of him.

"Hello, Lauren."

"Uh uh. Only my clients can call me Lauren. To you it's Lady Cunningham."

"Lady?"

She shoved an enormous heart-shaped diamond in his face, wiggling her finger so it blinded him.

Brett pulled together the last shred of his dignity. "Congratulations. Now, do you mind? I'm on my way out."

"Can't cut it around all the real stars, can we? I suppose they start asking uncomfortable questions. Speaking of which, how is that second script coming along?" Lauren smirked, shaking her head in mock pity.

Brett scowled back but couldn't argue. Lauren had every right to be mad at him. As his agent, she'd had access to Stanton Enterprises, only to have her connections ripped away during his crushing descent. He owed her money, time, and pieces of her life that he could never pay back. He just couldn't deal with that right now.

"Lau— Lady Cunningham. Can we please not go into this? I'm trying to catch someone before they leave."

Lauren moved the tiniest fraction to the left on her razor-sharp heels. "Oh yes, I'm sure you have an incredibly busy schedule. Let's just hope our paths don't cross again."

*Walk away. Don't say anything. Just walk away. And for fuck's sake, stop talking to yourself. You're a grown-ass man.*

Brett pushed past Lauren, not meeting her eyes. If he had, he'd have told her to shove her stupid stiletto up her stupid, smart ass. As if it would fit after that much liposuction.

Outside the party, the air was a whole barometric pressure unit lighter—free of the pounds of designer perfume and signature cologne. The lobby was also, however, free of Michel.

"I bet he left," Brett muttered.

The well-dressed man at the front desk looked up. "Can I help you, sir?"

Brett glanced around, checking for stray paparazzi. The black and white modernist entryway was free of cameras. "Could you tell me if Michel Polce is staying here?"

The man didn't blink. "I'm afraid no one by that name is staying at the hotel this evening."

"Dammit." Brett racked his brain. His sluggish, drunk brain. *Code names, codes names. If Michel was going to check in under a code name, what the hell would it be? A main character in one of his films? Too obvious. Nothing in popular media; Michel wouldn't risk it. What is the last name anyone would ask about at the front desk of the Bonne?*

Brett closed his eyes for a moment to stop the slight spinning and turned back to the blank-faced man behind the desk.

"Yes? Do you have another request, sir?"

"Yeah, my name is Brett Jacobs and I seem to have forgotten my room number. Could you remind me which one it is?" Brett asked, his voice flat. He produced his ID and swayed a little to add credibility to the claim that he was sufficiently drunk enough to be lost.

After examining his ID briefly, the man handed it back to him. "Suite 4018, Mr. Jacobs. It is on your room key."

Brett hung his head. "Right, yes. Thank you."

Of course it'd be his name. No one would ever expect the disgraced screenwriter, the laughing stock of the business, to be staying at a hotel whose nightly rates were higher than the cost of a five-bedroom house in Nebraska.

Lucille leaned against the balcony railing, casually contemplating what it'd be like to fall off the edge.

*Would people notice when I splat in their midst? Or would they chalk it up to another heiress gone off her meds? That's all I am to these people. A rich, snobby heiress who gets invited to these things because of who they believe my family is.*

*That's not fair. That's what I let them believe, and they're just too self-absorbed to see through it. God, I'm bored.*

If this mysterious client didn't show up soon, she was leaving. Like all the others, this event was ridiculous, dull, and shallow, and she was busy. Still, she liked having Raphael owe her.

"Lucille Anton?"

She turned to find a tall, tanned, dark-haired man in a sleek designer suit standing a few feet away and staring at her intently. She recognized him at once. His face was plastered all over the media as the forerunner for hottest man in the world. She glanced around. There were a few other people on the balcony, but their faces were glued to each other's like kids at prom.

"Can I help you?" she asked, feigning innocence. Raphael's speech was about to begin. That was the other reason she'd come: to hear one of Raphael's riot-provoking orations. She loved seeing the sycophantic crowd's awe transform into uncomfortable horror.

"I'm supposed to meet you here?" He had an accent, slight, but enough to cause the women of the world to collectively swoon. For sex on a stick, though, he seemed incredibly nervous.

"Yeah. Right." *Real professional, Lucille. Pull yourself together, woman!*

He grabbed her arm like he thought she might leave. "No, wait, Raphael told me to see you. He set this up."

Lucille's skin tingled under his broad hand. He was her meeting. She stepped back, out of his touch, to pull herself together. When she had, she extended her hand with all the casual grace she didn't feel. "Lucille Anton."

The man's smile could melt a glacier, his full lips parting to reveal straight white teeth. His deep brown eyes lit up as though Lucille was the most beautiful, charming woman on the planet and he wouldn't want to be anywhere but right there at that moment. Lucille felt her heart jump on impact.

"Michel Polce," he said, reaching out his hand to clasp hers.

# Chapter Three

*M*ichel *fucking* Polce, Lucille thought as his hand closed around hers. Of course she knew who he was—she doubted there was anyone left in the world who didn't. He was an internationally acclaimed, award-winning actor, director, screenwriter, producer, musician, designer, and all around media darling. He'd once hosted a reality TV show and all the contestants were eliminated in the first episode after spending the entire time fawning over him. Last year he'd published a book that was just half naked photos of himself and it'd been an overnight, runaway bestseller.

Of course, Lucille knew all this second hand. She'd never read, seen, or heard any of his work. She didn't have that kind of time.

But she knew a profitable client when she saw one, and Michel reeked of money, fame, and desperation. His black tux was custom made, his diamond-studded gold watch handcrafted. Everything about him spoke of outrageous amounts of disposable income. Broad and muscular, he had a physique no one as busy as him could achieve.

*He doesn't need to work out. With the kind of money he makes, he could pay someone to work out for him.*

This was not the time to think about his beautiful, perfect body. Something was upsetting Michel, something he'd come to her for help with. Her only interest in the man was what he needed from her and how much that assistance was worth.

"Perhaps we should go somewhere more private?" Lucille suggested in a soft purr. The balcony was too exposed for the kind of discussion they were about to have.

Michel's gaze flicked around the space before he replied. "Right, yes. I have a suite," he stated, as if having a room at the most expensive, exclusive hotel in the city was a given.

Lucille led the way out of the ballroom. When they reached the elevator, she turned to discover Michel had donned a black mask that covered half of his face like some sort of swashbuckling pirate. She raised her eyebrow at him.

"So no one will recognize me," he whispered.

Lucille's eyebrow crept higher.

"It worked on the way in."

*People in this town are dumber than I thought.* The elevator crept higher. "I thought you owned a house in Hills, Mr. Polce?"

Michel shifted. "I do. Of late it has become...convenient for me to keep a room here too."

Now Lucille's curiosity was on high alert. She had to know what had turned this suave megastar into a nervous wreck. And if that meant spending time alone with him in a hotel suite, then so be it.

It wasn't, in the basic sense of the word, a suite. A suite would have been a downgrade. Michel was staying in one of four exclusive apartments reserved for the uber rich, royalty, the president, and the pope. On the fortieth floor, they were admitted into a short hallway. Michel hurried her to his room, his eyes scanning the area. The door stuck, however, and required a hefty shove before it yielded enough to let them in. Once inside, Lucille saw the door's reluctance to open was the result of someone having shoved a large armchair in its way. This was not the only eccentricity, either. The whole room was, in fact, barricaded from within. The seating area had been stripped of all furniture save a solid black coffee table. A leather couch was wedged in the entrance to the adjoining bedroom. In front of each floor-length French door sat a white armchair, blocking access to the patio and its stunning city skyline view. A leather loveseat had been dragged inexplicably in front of the huge TV screen on the left-hand wall. Directly to the right of where she stood was a marble bar, the only part of the room that hadn't been dismantled.

Lucille took note of this with bland interest. Michel was insane; most of her clients were. Now it was a matter of seeing whether his insanity was something she could work with.

"Expecting someone, Mr. Polce?" she asked.

"Please, call me Michel," he said, ignoring her question. He was checking beneath the couches, behind the curtains, and even under the bar, in a methodical frenzy.

"Hmm." Lucille nodded.

Michel paused, his head almost under a chair, and turned to meet her eye. He flushed and asked, "Would you care for a drink, Ms. Anton?"

"Lucille. Club soda with lemon. Thank you." As she spoke, she strolled to one of the bar stools. It was bolted to the floor, which explained why it hadn't been sacrificed to the barricade. She never drank during client meetings. Alcohol loosened the tongue, something she counted on but couldn't indulge in. As she sat, she crossed one leg over the other, stretching the tight dress to its limit. This caused the Spanx to press on her bladder. She uncrossed her leg. This was not a situation in which she felt she could leave her new client alone, even to use the bathroom. "Shall we get started? I'd like to know where you heard of me."

Michel slid behind the bar and, with a flourish, poured her drink and a generous glass of whiskey for himself. As Lucille took a small sip from her glass, Michel downed his in one long swig and poured another. He met her gaze with deep brown, intense eyes.

"You must get a lot of solicitations."

She shrugged. He went on.

"Which is curious, because no one knows who you are or how to find you. How do you manage that kind of anonymity?" He went on without an answer. "No, don't tell me. Keep your secrets. You see, I've found myself in an...awkward situation of late."

He paused, staring at nothing. "Raphael knows. He told me to find you and that you could help me. But he didn't elaborate, so I'm intrigued—what is it you do?"

Lucille waited to see if he'd keep talking. When he didn't, she launched into her speech. "I'm a sort of spin doctor, but for celebrities. My clients are people who've done or said something they want to hide, and that's where I come in. I help them with the cover up, I manage their media image, and I protect their reputation."

Michel's eyes lit up as she spoke, and he leaned toward her. "Yes! That's what I need."

There was more, a whole history of how her Uncle Simon had started the business to meet the need for personalized celebrity image protection services, how stars had flocked to him, and now her, to guard them from their own career-threatening mistakes. *We make lying, cheating, nut-job celebrities look like caring, well-intentioned individuals. I am, in fact, a miracle worker,* she didn't say.

"Great. Now why don't you tell me more about your difficult situation and I'll tell you how I can help."

Michel's smile slid from his face. He deflated against the bar. "I'm afraid it isn't a simple one. The situation is...complicated."

"I'll decide that." Lucille was rarely rattled after eight years of such confessions.

Michel took a deep, exaggerated breath, the movement causing a piece of dark hair to fall over his eyes. "Two years ago, my life changed forever when I saw Sylvia Stanton. I was meeting with my producer to protest the title change of my third film, when in glides Sylvia, sweeping through the building like Athena riding into battle—terrifying and breathtaking."

*Christ, actors.*

He went on to depict Sylvia in precise sensory detail. Everything from the curl of her hair beside her left earlobe to the little sigh she gave when she put on a new pair of shoes. As Michel spoke, he paced the room, lost in memory. He described the first year and a half of their relationship in explicit detail. How inseparable and in love they were. How generous, kind, and supportive Sylvia was. How many times they'd banged on the side table in the entryway. Lucille cut him short when he launched into an exposition of how Sylvia tasted. She couldn't stomach it.

She resisted the temptation to look Sylvia Stanton up on her phone. Perhaps there were two women by that name. The Sylvia she knew of was spoiled, selfish, and obsessed with personal monetary gain.

"That all changed," Michel went on, a frown clouding his wistful recollections.

*Here it comes.*

"The moment I realized what she was."

*A colossal bitch?*

"She's trying to kill me."

Lucille choked on a sip of club soda. She forced herself to swallow, her eyes tearing as the carbonation caught in her throat. Swallowing again, she held back a cough, though the effort caused a few tears to fall. She wiped them away, hoping Michel hadn't noticed.

He hadn't. He was still talking, his back to her as he pulled aside a gauzy white curtain to stare into the dark night beyond.

"I can hardly believe it myself," he was saying.

"What did you say?" Lucille croaked.

"My fiancée is trying to kill me. Has been for some time." He spoke with flat detachment, devoid of his usual embellishment.

"But, what do you mean, she's trying to kill you?" She was asking dumb questions but couldn't help it. It wasn't every day a celebrity, and potential client, informed her that his fiancée wanted to murder him. "What's happened? What's she done?"

Michel turned to look at her, seeming to assess her, before continuing in the same flat, emotionless voice. "At first it might have been an accident. When I'm working on a film, I roam around the house with little heed to my surroundings. One afternoon, while acting out some dialogue, I tripped over Sylvia's suitcase, which had been left at the top of the stairs. I might have fallen down all forty-six stone steps, breaking my neck and each bone in my body on the way, but I grabbed the railing just in time. When I told Sylvia about it later, she apologized profusely and then was silent, sullen even, the rest of the night. Sylvia never stops talking, you see. I suppose I'll never know if that one was an accident or not, but I assure you, the next incident was intentional." He paused.

"Go on."

"I was walking through my gardens at the time cinematographers call the 'magic hour.' That last moment before the sun disappears beyond the horizon. When the sky glows red, orange, purple, and gold. Before the evening settles in with calm, graying dusk. I wandered slowly among the flowers as they prepared to close for the night. I paused to inspect a particularly vibrant leopard lily. From the periphery of my eye, I caught the flash of a camera. I straightened to get a better look. No sooner had I moved than a fifty-pound stone bust catapulted to the ground right where my head had been, taking the unsuspecting lily with it."

Lucille realized she'd been holding her breath, and exhaled slowly. She gulped her remaining drink, wishing it was whiskey, as she tried to think of how to respond.

Michel hadn't finished. "Since then, she's tried to poison and electrocute me as well."

"But how do you know she's the one doing this?"

"She hasn't exactly been subtle. She's never around when these things happen. And she's the only one who knows my creative process and the house well enough to set up these 'accidents.'"

Lucille stood, smoothed her dress, took a breath, and headed for the door. "Mr. Polce, I'm not sure what Raphael told you, but I don't cover up murders."

"Lucille—please don't leave." Michel grabbed her arm as she walked past him. "What are you talking about?"

"You're about to tell me you took matters into your own hands and murdered Miss Stanton. I'm saying I don't want any part in it."

Michel released her and frowned. "Kill Sylvia? Why would I kill Sylvia?"

*Wait, what?* "You haven't?"

"Never. I'd never kill her or hurt her or leave her. I love her," Michel said passionately.

"Oh." She exhaled in relief. This was a crazy she could handle.

"Lucille, how could you think I could... You thought I wanted you to..." The unspoken words hung in the air between them.

"Oh no, not at all! I'm sorry, I misunderstood you. Of course you wouldn't, *couldn't*, do such a thing." Lucille gave him her most dazzling smile.

Michel relaxed. Then his shoulders slumped more and he sighed. "That was Raphael's reaction, too. He told me I should go straight to the police."

Lucille asked why the hell he hadn't.

"If only I could! But I can't do that to Sylvia, I can't have her arrested. I love her too much." In the dim light of the room, Michel appeared tired and haggard. Beneath his cultivated façade, dark circles stood out under each eye and weary lines framed his mouth.

Neither spoke. Michel seemed to be trying not to cry. He stared through the window to the bright city lights beyond.

Lucille was trying to come up with a plan. Of all the celebrities she'd handled, all of the drug problems and weird fetishes, nothing came close to the story Michel told. Now he was crying in front of her. Should she call the police? Or a therapist? Should she comfort him or tell him to stop the delusion and face reality? None of the options seemed appropriate for dealing with an emotionally unhinged celebrity she'd just met. And none of them would get her the job.

She went for the obvious. "What if she kills you?"

Michel sighed again and rubbed his hands over his face as he turned to Lucille. His eyes were red and a little puffy. "I have thought of that. Which is why I'm going to confront her, tell her what I know, and ask her to stop doing it."

"You haven't tried that already?"

"I couldn't find the words."

*I bet.* "But you think it'll work."

"What other choice do I have?" His voice broke.

Lucille could think of a whole list of choices but didn't share them. Although he hadn't directly said so, Michel obviously didn't have a death wish; otherwise, he wouldn't have turned his hotel room into a fortress. But that was his problem. She wasn't being hired to save his life.

"So, what is it you want from me?"

Michel crossed the room and sat on the adjacent stool, facing her. "I wasn't sure at first, not knowing much about you. But now it's all coming together. You see, last week, Sylvia cut the brakes in my

Ferrari. I hit a bush, totaled the car, yet emerged unharmed. My name, however, was slandered by the media." His voice was animated and hopeful as he recounted the traumatic incident. "I was accused of driving drunk, high, or both. Sylvia's murderous plots won't be contained to our property forever. With my new film coming out, I can't lose fans over a falsely diagnosed drinking problem. Therefore, until I can convince her to stop trying to murder me, I want you to keep all this a secret. You protect Raphael's reputation—no small task. I want you to do the same for me."

That was when the pounding and shouting began.

They both jumped, the intensity broken.

Lucille expected, given his psychotic reorganization of the room, that Michel would handle the intruder with equally profound derangement. Instead, Michel broke off his wild-eyed panic and frowned at the door.

"That voice..." he mumbled to himself.

She watched in shock and horror, certain she was about to see Michel cut down at the height of his career, as he strolled to the door, unlocked it, and threw it open. A slovenly dressed man crashed into the suite.

"A period piece, no less!" the man shouted in a rousing finale.

# CHAPTER FOUR

B rett had been prowling the halls for some time. There were a ridiculous number of floors in the hotel, and after draining the flask in his jacket pocket, he was too drunk to read the numbers. He traced a brass shape that he'd been certain was a four but was actually a six, his mind wallowing in his failure and the pointlessness of life.

After Michel had taken up dating Sylvia, Brett had seen less and less of his supposed best friend. They'd severed all ties once the couple had moved to their villa in the Hills. Brett was left to drink his way from one side of the city to the other, alone. When he was a little drunk, he regaled unsuspecting bar patrons with tales of the former best friend who'd thrown him over for a woman. When he was very drunk, close to blacking out, he told the unwilling listeners about his screenplays; the mediocre, spectacularly unsuccessful first, *The Night Before the Apocalypse,* and the half-finished, untitled, stymied sequel. Only he'd start at the beginning, the very beginning, of his life. There were his stories of growing up in Chicago, the forgotten middle child in a house of high-functioning alcoholic artists. His siblings had thrived in the chaos and welcomed the revolving door of guests his parents entertained. Brett, a quiet child interested only in his science experiments and comic books, didn't fit. After thoroughly disappointing his family by getting a PhD in chemistry, he'd moved to LA, determined to write a blockbuster. But he was no writer and it took all his familial influence to get Stanton Enterprises to make his smashing failure of a film. To make matters worse, he couldn't write a second script to save his life. Brett would then dissolve into tears and hiccups, too overcome with his own failure to go into the subsequent blowout that had resulted in him losing his contract with Stanton, getting dropped by his agent, and being disowned by his family. Alone and rejected at thirty-two.

At this point someone, in a desperate attempt to shut him up, would call him a cab and send him home. He often woke on the front steps of his apartment building with a throbbing head and a fuzzy memory. Sometimes he'd find himself in bed with a strange, much-younger woman who inevitably proclaimed herself to be a huge fan of his work. A little fame went a long way with the twenty-somethings, and that was exactly what Brett had. A little fame.

Lately, between the drinking and the persistent failures, he'd felt himself slipping. He wanted to talk to Michel, rather than face his condescending family or try to resolve the issues with his therapist. Now even Michel had abandoned him. He was stuck alone in a hotel, at a party for an actor turned writer/director who'd had the audacity to make a fucking period piece.

Finally, he reached the right floor and stumbled his way to what he hoped was suite 4002. He pounded on the door, yelling, "Michel! I know it's you. That's a shitty way...supposed best friend. Invite them to a party...leave them...at fucking movie party...for a period piece, no less!"

At the last part of his speech, the door opened, and Michel yanked Brett into the room and slammed it shut behind him.

"Brett," Michel demanded, "what the hell are you doing here?"

Brett wanted to give Michel a piece of his mind—he'd been rehearsing the speech the whole night, and it was a showstopper. Before he could launch into his oration, he caught sight of long legs, dark hair, and a plunging neckline. A woman who definitely wasn't Sylvia eyed him from the bar with icy curiosity that sent shivers all over his body.

"You invited me," Brett said, his intoxicated brain struggling to process the scene before him. The combination of alcohol and his strong Midwestern accent made his words come out in a slurred stream of syllables. All that planning and pontificating, and this is what his bristled retort had become—*you invited me.*

"You never responded, so I assumed you weren't coming."

Brett fought his bow tie, which was strangling him. He couldn't stop looking at the woman, couldn't break his gaze away from her...everything. "There was something I wanted to talk to you about, as it turns out. But you're busy, so I'll just go."

He tore his eyes away from the woman, whipped around to stalk off, lost his balance, and plunked into the armchair sitting beside the door. When he looked up, Michel was watching him with bemused pity.

"You aren't going anywhere, my friend. Besides, Ms. Anton and I were just finishing our business meeting. Ms. Anton, Brett Jacobs, Sylvia's cousin and my dearest friend. Brett, Lucille Anton, my new publicist."

Lucille raised an eyebrow as she looked Brett slowly up and down. He felt naked. "Pleasure to meet you, Mr. Jacobs."

"Why do you have a new publicist?" Brett demanded, once again staring at Lucille. She was too put together. From her form-fitting, strapless red dress to her deep-red lips and smooth, lightly tanned skin, she was stunning. Yet, under that austere perfection, she radiated cold and unapproachable. He would have avoided her and her icy gaze had she not now stood between him and a clear conscience. As it was, Brett had a strong urge to mess up her dark, styled hair just to see how she'd react. "What happened to Grant?"

"I still have Grant."

"What? You're so famous you need two publicists? One won't cut it anymore?"

"Ms. Anton is a...specific type of publicist. More of an image designer than anything," Michel replied.

Brett tried to scrutinize them both at once but stopped when it made his head spin. Something was up, but neither party was giving away anything.

"I have everything I need here." Lucille broke the silence as she stepped forward to shake Michel's hand. "I'll stop by here with the contract tomorrow, Mr. Polce."

Michel smiled, his chin trembling. "You'll help?"

"Of course." Lucille returned the smile as Michel kissed her hand in gratitude. When she turned to Brett, her smile turned to a smirk. "It was...interesting meeting you, Mr. Jacobs."

Brett tried to respond but it came out as a jumbled mess of nonsense.

Just as Lucille was about to leave, Michel announced, "Drop it at my house. I'm going home and Brett is coming with me."

"Why?" Brett asked as Lucille added, "Him?"

Brett bit back the temptation to stick out his tongue at her.

Michel went on, ignoring their reactions. "I would feel safer having someone around at all times."

Either Brett was further gone than he'd thought or Michel was making no sense at all. *How the hell would having me there make him feel safer? Security guards make someone feel safe. I make them feel... I am not having a slumber party. I'm not a thirteen-year-old girl.*

Before he could make these protests out loud, Michel said, "Besides, your apartment is such a shit hole."

"Hey." Brett aimed a kick at him that Michel dodged. That was his bachelor pad Michel was dissing.

"Great. All settled. Brett, you'll move in in the morning."

*In the morning!* It already was morning, or close to it. This time it was Lucille who prevented his indignant protest.

"How about I bring the papers by around two?" she said, her expression inscrutable.

Michel nodded.

She left then, and the moment the door closed behind her, Brett turned to his friend and demanded, "Just what the hell is going on here?"

Brett stumbled back to his apartment, still congratulating himself on making it home before the sun rose. When he'd left the hotel, he'd declined Michel's offer of a ride, saying he needed time to clear his head—in other words, drink more without his friend seeing. But if he knew said friend at all, Michel would be there at dawn with a limo and no patience.

All the things Michel had told him had been running riot in his brain. A murderous fiancée, and not just any fiancée but Michel's specifically, and his cousin in particular. And a celebrity spin doctor, a title that was one hundred percent made up, riding in to save the day. But it had only taken a few minutes in a barricaded hotel room and this woman had Michel following her lead. Brett had no doubts about her being a badass, and possibly the badass who could keep his only friend from getting himself killed. He'd been mad at Michel and drunk and he really should try to get her on his side in this, just as soon as he could think about her without getting an instant boner.

Brett struggled with the lock. It gave way with a groan. At least he'd drowned out the thoughts of Lucille Anton's thighs around his waist, her body smashed against his. He'd had less success getting the other fantasies to leave. Those strong-willed alpha types always got him. His therapist said it was because he'd grown up without a strong maternal influence.

Whatever the reason, he hoped it would only take a few minutes alone in his unwashed sheets to cure him of it. As he mentally unzipped that red dress, he tripped over something hard and immobile and went sprawling on the floor.

"Brett, is that you?" Michel's voice said from somewhere nearby.

Brett rolled over and regretted the motion. His head spun and ached where he'd smacked it on the ground. And because of his thoughts as he stumbled into the room, his crotch had taken some of the fall as well. He curled into a fetal position on the wood floor as the lights switched on.

Michel sat in an armchair in the center of the trashed living space, blinking the sleep from his eyes. He was still put together, without a single wrinkle or a hair out of place, even after sleeping upright.

"What are you doing here, Michel?" Brett groaned.

"I came to get you. You weren't home yet, so I fell asleep while I waited," Michel said with a deep, abandoned look.

"Normal people take the bed. Or text their friend to tell them they're breaking in and waiting," Brett mumbled, his words sliding together despite his best intentions.

"There's a pile of dirty dishes and books in your bed. And I did text you, like twenty times."

"Oh."

"Yeah. Oh." Michel waited ten seconds, then asked, "Are you ready to go?"

Brett let out another groan. "It's five in the morning. I just got home, as you saw. Now my head hurts and my dick's killing me. Do you really think I'm ready to go?"

"Why's your dick killing you?"

Brett tried to think through the fog. "What? Oh hell, never mind. I'm not ready."

Michel stood and brushed invisible lint off his suit. "Hurry up. I don't think I can stand this hell hole a minute longer."

"Hey. This hell hole is my home."

"There are dirty socks on the lampshade and whiskey bottles in the flower pots. You're using the *Times* as toilet paper."

"I hate the *Times*," Brett grumbled.

Yes, he lived in a stinky refuse heap of an apartment, but he didn't appreciate Michel barging in to comment on it. He regretted agreeing to this plan already. While Brett had been trampled by criticism and rejection, falling into his current sloven state, Michel had been living it up with the jet set. Now Brett was jumping to his friend's aid as though nothing had happened. That, more than the mold-caked plates in his bed and the rotting food in his fridge, made him feel disgusting.

"You can't just barge in here and demand I leave immediately. What if I have important things to do today?"

"Like what, Brett?"

Brett wanted a great comeback. He wanted Michel to regret abandoning him. His head hurt. His dick smarted. "Like...write."

"Brett." Michel's gaze was sympathetic. "We both know you aren't working on the screenplay. There's a huge spider web over your desk chair."

Brett didn't respond.

"Come on, man. Get off the floor."

When Brett didn't move, Michel sighed. "Look, I know I haven't been around a lot lately. I had no idea things had gotten so bad here. I'm sorry. But I'm here now and I need your help, okay?"

Michel sounded so hopeful and so unlike his dramatic, neurotic self that Brett tilted his head to look at his friend. He wasn't sure whether he believed Michel or not, but he wanted to. He wanted Michel to be sorry and for them to go back to the way things were. If he were honest, which he rarely was, Brett was afraid of himself, of the person who drank to keep the darkness of his own failure at bay. He climbed slowly to his feet and headed to his bedroom to pack.

Michel followed him. "What do you think of Lucille?"

Brett rubbed his face and looked around for a suitcase. It was somewhere in the foot-deep sea of shit on his floor. "I don't know about her. A spin doctor for celebrities? Doesn't that sound a little suspicious to you?"

"Raphael highly recommended her. Besides, what choice do I have?"

*Tons. Tons of choices, Brett wanted to yell. You could literally do a hundred other things besides hire a sexy woman with a made-up job.*

Instead he said, "If you think she can help, I say it's worth a try. She is really hot."

He hadn't meant to say the last part out loud. *Blame it on the alcohol.*

"Don't fuck her."

Brett put on a look of total innocence. "I didn't mean it like that—"

"I'm serious. If you don't listen to another word I say, fine. Don't fuck her. I need this woman's help." Michel's eyes were stormy and cold.

"The same goes for you."

"I'm a one-woman man."

"Yeah, one crazy murderous bitch."

"Hey. She's *my* crazy murderous bitch. Now promise me you won't fuck Lucille Anton."

Brett raised his hands in defeat. "All right, all right, I promise."

# Chapter Five

As she sat in her office, Lucille didn't waste a single thought on one of the two men she'd met the night before. All her attention was focused on the other, the powerful, fragile man who needed her help. Michel was the most challenging, thrilling case she'd ever encountered, and her first move had to be perfect.

Even before Brett's interruption, Lucille had known she'd accept Michel's case. She'd grown bored with her typical clients. A person could only spend so much time helping teenage TV stars save face with their preteen fan clubs. She'd helped rappers keep their disreputable image, "it" couples maintain the charade after they broke up, and the truly tortured artists only appear tortured. But her résumé didn't include a three-time winner of America's Sexiest Man Alive who wanted to keep his heiress fiancée's murderous schemes under wraps.

That Michel, an intelligent though neurotic man, would make the conscious decision to stay with a woman who wanted him dead was intriguing.

Well, maybe she did think about Brett Jacobs for a minute. Or an hour. Or whenever she tried to focus on her work. The man was hot, in the completely opposite way Michel was hot. Michel was sexy and rich without a hair out of place. Brett was…a mess. His suit well-tailored but wrinkled, the top buttons of his shirt undone under his knot of a bow tie and his hair falling hopelessly over his eyes. He wasn't muscular and his face had the haunted look of too many late nights. But the way he crashed into the room, not giving a damn what anyone thought, determined to save his friend at all costs, that was the sexiest thing Lucille had ever seen. She tried and failed to stop imagining what he looked like naked.

She pushed her thoughts of both men aside and got down to the real problem at hand, Sylvia Stanton.

It took her all morning to research Sylvia. As the only child of Lou Stanton and his first wife, whose name no one remembered, Sylvia was set to inherit millions, maybe more. Millions that were tied up in the vast holdings of Stanton Enterprises and guarded carefully by her father. However, party girl

Sylvia didn't seem to want to be a CEO, given that her activities were largely composed of throwing drinks at people in public places, giving interviews about her eating habits, and being a celebrity judge at modeling competitions. She was well known in her own right, but her relationship with Michel had made her status soar and even, Lucille suspected, spiral out of control.

There were articles on Sylvia and Michel, on every outfit she'd ever worn anywhere, and on the fights she'd started with other women, most notably her feud with Reina Winter. Then the story she'd been looking for popped up on her laptop as she sipped the last spice-laden dregs of her quad-shot, skinny, extra-dry cappuccino with a sprinkle of cinnamon between the espresso and milk. In the screaming pink headlines of a three-month-old *Just Like Us* magazine was an article about Sylvia. Prominently centered below the title "Daddy's Little Girl Disowned" was a huge photo showing the Stanton Enterprises heiress strolling along the beach in a string bikini, her long blonde hair dancing across her tanned face. While the picture was flattering, the story was anything but. Sylvia, reportedly, had gone to her father for money. Negotiations had turned into a verbal blowout in the crowded bar of the Stanton Suites Hotel. A witness had filmed the debacle, and the video had gone viral within the hour. Lucille watched the linked footage eight times—for research purposes, of course. It was an ugly fight. Sylvia pouted like a preteen, while the normally laconic Lou Stanton threatened to cut her off without a credit card and have everyone in the place arrested if they didn't fuck off immediately. Finally, after smashing several martini glasses, Sylvia stormed out, vowing never to speak to her father again. The article speculated on why Sylvia hadn't gone to her rich fiancé for money instead.

Lucille had met Sylvia Stanton two years ago. She'd been attending the premiere of the latest blockbuster, written, directed, and produced by Michel Polce. Also starring Michel Polce, naturally. Her plan had been to gather intel for her new client, model Reina Winter, whose Swedish actor fiancé, Michel's co-star, had just been caught in bed with the entire production team. It was the year gold was in and so she'd worn gold, a simple, elegant dress, without showing much skin and no daring long sleeves or bold accessories. She had worn the perfect outfit to ensure she didn't end up on either the best- or worst-dressed lists for the night.

Sylvia Stanton, on the other hand, had topped the best of the best with her daring, skin-revealing navy gown designed personally for her by renowned recluse Martín Piero. The dress rippled around her as she flowed across the red carpet, graceful in her five-inch heels, her hand resting casually on Michel Polce's arm and her look one of pure, smug satisfaction.

Lucille, per usual, had slipped in the side and arrived just in time to watch this perfect pair flaunt their way into the post-screening ballroom. She'd stared at them; it was impossible not to. She hadn't been close enough to see their expressions, but she'd felt she could sense a shade of tension in Michel, a small sign that he wasn't quite comfortable being the center of so much unadulterated fawning. Sylvia, however, had looked around at the packed room of celebrities as though they were her subjects and she their queen.

But confirmation on why half of the room hated Sylvia and the other half envied her was not why Lucille had been there. As Michel had broken the spell in the room with a casual wave of his hand, Lucille had spotted Reina with her own gathering of adoring admirers, ninety-eight percent of whom were men. Which meant that the news of Reina's break up had got out. Which meant that Lucille had been there to find out if her plan had worked, if the public had bought her cultivated story as the truth.

An hour later she had been convinced they had. Reina had still been swamped with fans of the single male variety, and everyone, save his agent, had been giving her ex, Andreas, a wide berth. Lucille had smiled to herself and left without anyone noticing.

As she watched the video again, Lucille was struck by the difference the two years had made on the heiress. She was smaller, slimmer, and had lost that holier-than-thou posture. The woman in the video was desperate and vicious, which lent proof to Michel's claims.

Lucille thought of her options. If there was no way to keep the murder attempts secret, she'd have to leak the story, on her terms, with her spin. It would be easy to frame a jealous stalker fan gone mental. Michel had to have other people with motive to murder him. But whatever she came up with would have to explain Sylvia's disinheritance as well; otherwise, the fiancée would be the primary suspect.

Lucille's phone buzzed, reminding her of her noon lunch meeting with the very same Reina Winter. No doubt the model would have something to say about Sylvia Stanton.

"Excuse me. Do you have to put your chair there? No, no, don't bother moving. I'm only trying to get by. Oh, that's really mature. Yeah, you enjoy your lunch too, sir."

Lucille's fingers paused over her phone. Some idiot was bumbling through the crowded restaurant, pissing people off in his wake.

The café thrived on atmosphere. Everything from the pianist playing Chopin in the corner to the monosyllabic waiters in starched black and white spoke of prestige and intimate discretion. Being the noon hour, the small room was full. The primary clientele were men in dark business suits with matching ties and deep furrows in their brows. Some ate accompanied by smartphones and laptops so the physical necessity for food would not hinder their productivity. Others lunched with well-dressed clients, conducting business meetings with leisurely efficiency. The waiters slid between the tables, holding trays like extensions of their arms and never breaking their smiles. The Chopin meandered in the background, loud enough to be present without upsetting the intimate haven. Miachelli's was the mecca of the business lunch and the private tête-á-tête.

Now an ignorant troublemaker had splintered that artifice of calm elegance. An ignorant trouble-maker with a familiar voice. Lucille dismissed any recognition and returned to the pressing demands of her email.

Reina was late, and Lucille's patience wore thin over the caprese salad. If Reina weren't an ob-scenely rich, colossally dysfunctional model, Lucille wouldn't bother waiting. Punctuality was her un-breakable rule, yet, with the right combination of fame, wealth, and chronic issues, she'd overlook it.

Three things happened at once. Lucille hit send on an email to a prospective client, her stomach rumbled in hungry protest, and she looked up to find the obnoxious gatecrasher standing over her, wearing a ferocious scowl.

"Can I help you?" she asked the man. That her heart jumped when she saw him only annoyed her more.

"You don't remember me from yesterday," Brett said.

"I remember you. Mr....Jacobs, yes? That doesn't explain why you're interrupting my lunch." Lucille knew she was playing her ice-queen-bitch role, but dammit, the man was a hot mess and his gaze made her want to squirm in her chair.

Brett took her words as an invitation and helped himself to the chair across the table. He ignored the glares from the indignant diners he'd upset and leaned over the pristine white china to scowl more at Lucille.

Unlike the well-dressed patrons of the restaurant, Brett wore last night's clothes. His jacket gaped open. His bow tie had become a limp scrap of silk that hung about his neck. His shirt was more wrinkled than before and sported a light stain on the left collar. The deep spice of whiskey assailed Lucille's nostrils as he leaned closer. His dark hair stuck out in a disheveled mess of poorly applied product and unbrushed mayhem. The stubble around his jaw was scruffy and unkempt, yet his blue eyes were sharp, lucid, and intent on hers.

Lucille had to look away before he could read the interest she couldn't hide. She let her breath out slowly, her gaze sweeping the room. She spied the maître d' shifting uncomfortably by the door, his gaze flicking to Brett. *Why hasn't the man dealt with the situation already?*

"Excellent. We're on the same page then, Ms. Anton."

"What page would that be?"

"We both remember each other. Meaning we must have made a strong, repugnant impression on one another. Same page."

*Yes, I find you totally...repugnant.*

"Look, Mr. Jacobs, I am about to have an important, *private* meeting with someone, and your rude intrusion is very unwelcome. If you are seeking representation, email me, don't stalk me. But you should know I'm not currently accepting clients, and even if I was, this"—she gestured to his appearance—"wouldn't increase your chances." Lucille gave Brett a long, withering, introspective look, lingering on the unknown collar stain and the ratted mess of hair. She returned to her email, thereby giving him what she felt was a firm invitation to go fuck himself. It was a cover, of course. Not even she could deny what that look had cost her composure. If she'd looked any longer she'd have banged him right there on the table, right on the starched white linen until they were both covered in expensive olive oil and were arrested for public indecency. The idea almost made her smile and fueled her annoyance with Mr. Brett Jacobs.

"I have a publicist."

"Not for much longer, I would think." Lucille didn't, couldn't, look up.

"If you're referring to my second film, it's coming out next year, and my publicist is well aware of that fact. If you had seen the first, you'd know—"

"I've seen it," Lucille cut him off. She wished he'd give up and leave. She wished the maître d' would stop skirting around the eyesore in his establishment and have Brett thrown out already. The man appeared to be a short, solid sort of waiter. The kind who was used to having his orders obeyed. At the moment, though, he was dithering, his mouth twitching beneath his mustache.

"You've seen my film?" Brett returned her attention to the matter at hand.

"Yes."

"So you understand why—"

"I hated it," she lied to shut him up. She loved his film, but she wasn't about to tell him that.

"You hated it?" Brett blinked, grasping for composure and missing. "But...what did you... I mean, you hated it?"

"I prefer my movies with less fluff and fantasy. It was utterly unrealistic. Besides, zombies are done. Stop reanimating them." *Now that is funny.* Though not as funny as how much he seemed to care what she thought about his work.

"Unrealistic? Zombies? You didn't see it," Brett sputtered, his face reddening. "Because if you had, you'd know the reanimation theme is a metaphor for—"

*And totally lost on him.* "I got it. You, Mr. Jacobs, are a cliché. A so-called visionary screenwriter who wrote a single mediocre script and now can't write the second to save his life. Wasting away on alcohol and mismanaged fame." It was a bitch move, but she needed him to leave before Reina arrived. Or before she grabbed his stupid, indignant face and made out with it. Besides, no one had ever accused her of being a people person.

Brett gulped, his face scarlet. "But. But—"

"Mr. Jacobs. I am an incredibly busy woman. I can't sit here and argue cinematic merit with you. Nor do I wish to. I'm about to have an important meeting that you are not welcome at."

Brett found his voice again. "Your client is either invisible or very late. Since I doubt you believe in ghosts..."

Lucille bristled. "Your point?"

"I was about to make it."

"Then make it."

Brett didn't say anything right away. His face had gone back to a nice, normal color, but his eyes bit out anger. Lucille admired his persistence but loathed his timing.

"What are you doing with Michel?"

"As we covered last night, I have been contracted to help Mr. Polce with his media image." She never broke her icy stare. She did, however, push her breasts out. Because she could.

Brett's breath hitched, his gaze flicking to her cleavage before returning to her eyes. "You didn't blink once. You're lying through your teeth and you didn't blink. Impressive. But let's get something straight. I know about Sylvia, I know what she's trying to do, and I know Michel needs to go to the police, not you. I know you know all of this too. So, I'll ask you again, who are you and what are you doing with Michel?"

Lucille narrowed her eyes at him. She felt cornered and wanted to pounce, but she'd already used her attack. She'd thrown her underhanded punches, hoping to enrage his self-eviscerating inner critic, but he hadn't budged. Michel had told Brett her true identity, that was clear, but the annoyingly cute, scruffy asshole was trying to trick her into admitting her bluff. She didn't know what his angle was and was starting to realize she cared. It was time for a new tactic.

Her eyes softened and she smiled. "Can I call you Brett? Brett, I'm afraid you've been misinformed. I've only been hired to help with his media image. I've never met Michel before last night. All I know is what my client tells me, and I have no idea what you're referring to."

Brett watched her. "Oh, you are good. Now you're trying to, what, make me out as a delusional nutcase? I may end up dying alone in a mental ward from cirrhosis of the liver, but I know I'm right about this."

*Writers. Always so damn dramatic.* She suppressed a laugh and gave him an extra glare for making her laugh when she was irritated.

"You're right about what?" she asked, baiting him.

"I'm right that Sylvia is trying to kill Michel. I'm right that whoever you are and whatever you're doing, it isn't being his fucking PR manager. I'm right that someone needs to arrest the deranged bitch before she actually succeeds in murdering him." Brett was breathing heavily. With each statement, he'd bent closer to Lucille, stopping inches from her face. In the process, he'd dragged the sleeve of his jacket through the forgotten caprese salad, and olive oil dripped onto the spotless white tablecloth. "You're an intelligent woman. But you're remarkably misguided if you think whatever you're doing will help save Michel's goddamn life."

Lucille boiled. She hadn't been attacked so vehemently since Simon's trial, and the unbridled rage that had surfaced then was returning for an encore. Brett was close enough for her to kiss him or punch him, and at the moment both were likely.

The previously inattentive waiter chose that moment to arrive with what he likely felt was a casual proposition.

"Would sir and madam care to place an order?"

The vicious snarls he received in reply were, he clearly felt, entirely unwarranted, and he hurried away, no doubt thoroughly discouraged about the prospect of a good tip.

On his heels arrived the long-awaited lunch companion. She was not so easily dismissed.

"Lucille! Darling, terribly sorry I'm late. Oh, hello. Will you be joining us?" Reina Winter floated to the table in spiky, nude stilettos, wearing what resembled a burlap sack draped across her tall, thin body in cascading beige folds. Though the restaurant patrons had ignored the heated discussion between the rude man and the unobtrusive woman, every eye turned at Reina's entrance. She had that kind of appeal. The rebuffed waiter hovered nearby, just staring at Reina.

Lucille stood, clasped the model's outstretched hands, and kissed her on each cheek. Internally, she seethed, but externally, she snapped into professional detachment. "Reina. Not a problem. Don't bother with Mr. Jacobs, he was just leaving."

Reina turned to Brett, who stood glaring at Lucille. "Lovely to meet you, Mr. Jacobs," she purred, kissing him on either cheek. "I'm—"

"Reina Winter," Brett mumbled. His face flushed and he spoke with some difficulty. No man on earth, no human on earth, was immune to Reina. Lucille, who considered herself immune to everyone, had blushed more than once in the presence of her enchanting client. That didn't stop the stab of jealousy she felt at Brett's reaction to Reina.

Brett turned back to Lucille. "I'll see you later."

Before she could protest, he strolled through the restaurant. By the door he was stopped by the nervous maître d' who, still sweating and twitching, whispered something in the Brett's ear. Brett nodded, scribbled his autograph on one of the starched cloth napkins, and left.

Lucille, watching these events while Reina flirted with the hapless waiter, wanted to throw something at him. Something heavy so it'd hurt a lot. Because goddammit, he had a cute butt.

# CHAPTER SIX

B rett didn't know what had possessed him to show up at the restaurant. After his stuff had been forcibly moved to Michel's house, he'd once more declined the ride offer, saying he'd sleep off his hangover and wander over later. He'd needed to clear his head, which had throbbed from extended mental and physical abuse. He'd lain on his bed between his beloved chemistry texts, but his brain had refused to sleep. Perhaps he'd drank too much. That didn't seem likely. Perhaps he'd gotten a concussion when he'd face-planted.

He'd considered calling Michel and demanding a ride to the hospital, but he'd had no idea where his phone was.

An unproductive few hours later, Brett had dragged himself out of his crackling sheets and set off on the long pilgrimage to Michel's mansion. He'd decided to walk as far as he could, determined to refresh himself with some smog-filled air. An hour of that nonsense had convinced him he needed to find Lucille Anton and demand answers from her. It had been a coincidence when, a few blocks later, he'd caught sight of her through the window of Miachelli's. He'd been foolish enough at the time to believe it was luck.

He had intended to play nice. That was what he told himself. Then the dumb people with their obnoxiously spaced chairs and Lucille's general stuck-upishness...well, he might have overreacted a little. But she'd insulted his film, his beloved, terrible film, and things had gotten out of hand. It was her fault, her snobbish refusal to tell him the truth. Still, the whole encounter had left him feeling shitty.

Things were getting complicated, and the only way Brett knew to make sense of them was to write it all down. He grabbed a taxi and pulled his battered, tiny notebook out of his jacket pocket. In it he wrote:

*Michel: Acting strange. Victim of attempted murder. Wants me around. Won't go to the police because of stupid pig head.*

*Sylvia: Attempted murderer, apparently. Who knew? Motive? Money.*

*Lucille Anton: Hot ice queen (good song title). Supposed media image specialist. Actually has made-up job as undercover celebrity spin doctor.*

*Me: Caught up in all this. Very sober.*

It was starting to sound like a Shakespearean comedy. All they needed was a jester.

Brett amended his entry.

*Me: ~~Caught up in all this.~~ Very sober. Fucking jester.*

Perhaps he should start composing bawdy songs to perform at the king's feast. King Michel. The first would be "Hot Ice Queen."

The taxi pulled up outside Michel's mansion not a moment too soon. The house was a Spanish-style villa with a red shingled roof and beige concrete walls. Its grounds took up a city block, with an acre just for the circular tree-lined drive alone. The house danced the line between elegant and ostentatious, the latter often winning. There were rumors that Michel had bought the mansion from the don of a Spanish mafia clan and that there were bodies buried on the grounds. Michel had neither confirmed nor denied the rumor, so it was probably true.

Brett sighed at it. It gave him the creeps. He'd always hated staying there, preferring his noisy mess to the silent mausoleum.

As the taxi pulled away, the front door slammed open. Michel stood in the doorway, his hair crazed, his brown eyes wild, wearing the same suit as the night before. He didn't say a word, just stared at Brett like he was seeing a ghost. Brett had never seen him look so terrible.

"Jesus Christ, man, are you all right?"

Michel still didn't say anything, but he turned and stumbled into the house, Brett trailing behind him.

The pristine house was silent, eerily so. They walked through the cobblestone foyer where not so much as a speck of dust dared venture, their footsteps echoing against the vaulted ceilings. An enormous photograph hung on the wall beside the door, Michel with his arm around the blonde, ravishing woman whose villainous behavior had sparked this bromance reunion weekend. They both looked performance-ready and genuinely unhappy. Michel sighed at the portrait, then shifted his gaze to the second- and third-floor balconies that flanked the grand staircase, looking for something that wasn't there.

"Uh..." Brett tried again. "Michel? Where is everyone?" Normally he would have been greeted by the butler and seen at least two maids by this point. Michel kept his house staffed like an English estate.

"I sent them home," Michel said.

"Why?"

"I don't know who to trust, Brett." The same flat, emotionally dead voice.

Brett frowned as some pieces began fitting together. Michel had finally lost his mind. He'd known the pressure on his friend was enormous and that the man had been becoming more eccentric in the past few years, but now Michel had actually lost it and sent away the staff who'd been faithful to him for ages.

"Okay." Brett trod gently. "You don't know who to trust. Do you trust me?"

"She's gone." It was a whisper, a tiny, desperate whisper of a statement.

"Who's gone?"

"Sylvia." Michel's breath caught and his shoulders shook as he choked out the words. "She's gone. Someone took her. They stole into our house and took her while she slept."

Brett blinked at his friend, not understanding. He'd never been a big fan of his cousin, particularly since this new aspect of her personality had come to light, but kidnapped? Who *would want to kidnap Sylvia? Scratch that. Anyone. Everyone. Every-*

*one would want to kidnap her, and they wouldn't even need a good reason to do it.*

He grasped Michel's shoulders and steered him to a black leather couch in the sitting room. Michel collapsed, tears streaming down his face, his breath coming out in hiccups. Brett stood beside him, uncertain of what to say. He patted Michel on the arm, but even that felt stilted and weird, so he stopped.

Something stank of whiskey and dried sweat. No doubt the pleasant aroma was coming from his own body, the body he'd tortured over the past twenty-four hours. He wasn't fit to help anyone until he took a shower and figured out which room his clothes were in.

Whether Reina didn't notice the buzz around them or didn't care, Lucille wasn't certain. The model ranted as if nothing was happening while her highly paid publicist itched to reach for the phone chattering away in her purse. Lucille nodded along, reaching down as discreetly as possible to grab it. Stealing a glance, she saw it was littered with alerts from all the major news sites. Whatever was happening was big.

From the table beside theirs a woman said, "Did you read this? Sylvia Stanton's been kidnapped. She was taken from her home last night, it says."

"Who's Sylvia Stanton?" the man with her asked.

"You know, she's that rich business guy's daughter. The one who's engaged to Michel Polce."

Lucille froze, her attention disconnecting from Reina and tuning into the conversations around her.

"—missing since yesterday."

"—bet he did it."

"—she's loaded."

"—where was he? 'No comment'—what bullshit is that?"

"—I don't know what to do. Yes, he is in Sweden, but he knows how to find me." The last was from Reina, her eyes filling with the glistening tears of a beautiful crier.

"Reina," Lucille cut her off. "I have to go. I'm sorry. Have them put it on my tab." It would take her another hour to reach Michel's house in this traffic.

"Lucille! You can't just—"

She'd never run out on a client before. Scratch that. She'd frequently abandoned one client in favor of a more important one. If Sylvia Stanton had been kidnapped, there was precious little time before the media shit storm broke and Michel's name was caught in it. Kidnapping or not, Michel's reputation was being called into question, and that was her primary concern.

She had, however, never run out on Reina before. *If Reina had been on time,* she told herself, *we'd have had a chance to finish our entrees.* For once, she didn't care if she lost her client over this, and now was not the time to examine that unexpected reaction.

As Brett pulled a clean t-shirt over his head, the front doorbell rang. He ran his fingers through his wet hair—he hadn't thought to pack a brush. The bell rang again. Right. The butler was gone. The maids were gone. Who the hell knew where Michel's driver was. Michel was useless. Sylvia was supposedly kidnapped. He was the only semi-sane person in the place, so it looked like it was up to him to answer the door.

When he did, he found Lucille Anton standing on the other side of it, looking as beautiful and surly as she had at the restaurant.

"What the fuck is going on?"

"Hello to you, too," he said back, miffed. He'd only just started recovering from their last encounter; he wasn't ready for round two.

Lucille had her arms crossed over her black blouse, forcing open the unbuttoned top and revealing a glimpse of black lace. She looked him up and down while he stared at her face. He could feel her eyes on his skin, scraping across every inch of his being with slow, deliberate judgment. As in the hotel suite, he felt gloriously naked. He was sure it was meant to make him feel insignificant and tiny, but whether it was from his years of neuroses and self-deprecation or some latent desire in her gaze, he shivered with pleasure at the scrutiny.

"I see you own other clothes." Her tone was clipped and cold.

"Are you checking me out?" Brett had meant to joke, but it came out husky.

Lucille laughed, one brief, humorless bark that said "you wish." She pushed past him and into the tomb of the mansion beyond. She paused in the foyer, taking in the empty stillness.

"I don't know how to say this, but—" Brett began.

"Sylvia's been kidnapped." Lucille cut him off. "And what I'd really like to know is why the hell you didn't call me about it. You've clearly been here long enough to make yourself at home."

Brett frowned. "What does Sylvia's kidnapping have to do with you? Aren't you Michel's publicist?"

Lucille turned on her scary, pointy-heeled boots and glared at him, her arched eyebrows knit together. "Don't be stupid."

"Then you're not his publicist." Brett already knew this, of course, but he was annoyed and sick of her, and wildly attracted to her and now a bit pissed off.

"No. I'm not. We both know I'm not, so we can drop the charade. I need to see Michel." She turned and walked away, her heels ringing against the stone.

Brett growled after her. What was he, a wild animal? Now he was back to thinking about them having sex. Wild, passionate animal sex. He growled again.

The doorbell rang. "What the everlasting fuck?" he said as he wrenched it open.

On the terracotta doorstep stood three people Brett had been hoping they wouldn't have to deal with yet. The man in the middle was tall, a whole head taller than Brett. He wore a navy-blue suit, sunglasses, and the deep lines of a man with a stressful job. The two tall men flanking him, one ginger, one blond, were uniformed policemen. Which meant the middle man was...

"Detective Adams, LAPD," he said, confirming Brett's guess.

"Detective," Brett got out, voice croaking. He cleared his throat. "What can I do for you?"

"We need to speak to Mr. Polce," Detective Adams said, looking past Brett and into the house.

Brett hesitated. He knew Michel didn't want the police involved, but that was before Sylvia had been kidnapped and Michel himself had become weepy and catatonic. "He's in the living room." He motioned for the men to follow him.

The detective walked with slow deliberation, seeming to take in the deserted space around him. He nodded to the other cops and they followed him silently, their gaze roving over every detail of the room, no doubt looking for fingerprints or DNA samples. If Detective Adams pulled out a notebook and jotted down clues, Brett wouldn't be surprised.

"Hey guys, so, we've got company," he called as they strolled into the living room.

Lucille had pulled up a chair next to Michel's couch and had helped him into a sitting position. Michel was leaned forward, his head in his hands, and he didn't glance up when they entered. Lucille, on the other hand, looked up and caught sight of the detective. An expression flickered across her face and was gone before Brett could guess what it meant..

Brett frowned and glanced back at the detective. Detective Adams had stopped and was busy grinding his teeth and turning red.

"Lucy," he said, his voice gruff and masculine.

"Matt," Lucille replied, her face blank.

Brett felt lighter and grinned. This whole day was looking up. He leaned on the arm of the sofa. He was going to enjoy this. "So I take it you two know each other," he said, coaxing their claws out.

"We used to." Lucille still didn't look away from the detective.

The detective let out a short, cold bark of a laugh.

"What are you doing here, Matt?" Lucille's voice could have frozen a lake in July.

Detective Adams's mouth became a thin line, but he responded. "That's classified."

Lucille sighed. "Just make it easier on everyone and tell me. I'll find out anyway." She had her arms folded across her chest again, which made Brett sit up straighter.

"I need to question Mr. Polce about the whereabouts of his fiancée."

"He doesn't know where she is."

"Like I'd take your word for it, Lucy."

Matt the detective addressed Michel. "Mr. Polce, if you wouldn't mind stepping into another room for a moment, I have some questions for you."

Michel groaned, proving existence of life.

"Mr. Polce, this will go more smoothly if you co-operate."

Michel raised his head but didn't look at the detective. He met Brett's eyes first, his own red rimmed and desperate, pleading with him. Brett didn't know what Michel was pleading about and said so. Michel didn't respond, save to fix Lucille with his heart-wrenching gaze. Lucille broke away to look at Brett. For the first time, he saw something in her eyes that wasn't ice or fire. It wasn't businesslike detachment or irate fury. He saw something almost akin to sympathy.

The whole exchange lasted a few seconds. The emotion disappeared, and they broke their gaze.

"Mr. Polce—"

Lucille interrupted, "Matt, I need to talk to you. Right now."

Detective Adams protested, but Lucille grabbed his arm and dragged him into a side room. The door slammed behind them, and Brett was left behind, feeling like something hadn't gone according to plan.

# CHAPTER SEVEN

*What are you doing?* Lucille's brain demanded as the door slammed shut. *We don't get involved with the police or kidnapping or murderers. Especially when one of them is our ex-boyfriend. Oh, just shut up.*

Lucille had pulled them into a little kitchen of sorts. It was screened in, with a door leading out to the back patio. There was a huge grill along one side and a barbecue pit in the middle of the floor. A stocked bar curved out from the wall beside them. It smelled of campfire and tequila.

She crossed to the opposite side of the pit from Matt. The location didn't matter. What mattered was the man in the navy suit. The man she hadn't seen in eight years.

His hair, his beautiful brown hair, had streaks of gray in it. His face showed the strain of the job.

"Detective, huh?"

He scowled. "I don't want to make small talk with you. I have work to do. Say what you're going to say so I can get back to it."

"Fine. This is my case. Mr. Polce is my client. Stay the fuck out of it." She kept her manner calm and her words forceful.

Matt scowled more. "Lucy, you can't honestly tell me you've involved yourself in a kidnapping case."

"Of course I haven't. As I said, Mr. Polce is my client. He doesn't want the police involved in his life, and I am in charge of making sure his wishes are seen to, got it?" Before Matt could react, she added, "And don't call me Lucy."

"Mr. Polce is the key witness in the Stanton kidnapping case. I could have you arrested for obstruction of justice."

"Sylvia Stanton hasn't even been gone twenty-four hours. How can you call it a kidnapping case?" Lucille shot back.

"Because her father is Lou Stanton." He didn't need to say more. Estranged or not, if Lou Stanton wanted his daughter back, he'd turn the whole city upside down, rules and regulations be damned. "He got an anonymous threat this morning, demanding ransom for his missing daughter and implicating Mr. Polce was the perpetrator."

Lucille sighed. "I can tell you for a fact that Mr. Polce is innocent of the kidnapping."

Matt didn't react.

"He has been in the city with me and/or Mr. Jacobs since yesterday evening."

Matt raised an eyebrow. She knew from her intimate knowledge of him that he was looking her over for any signs of perjury.

"Your word is useless, Lucy. You lie for a living," he said.

"Not about the things that matter." She filled her words with meaning, injecting them with the memories of their relationship—two naïve romantics, playing at forever.

Matt sighed. "I can't stop the investigation."

"Good, I don't want you to. You're right, I don't get involved with kidnappings, and someone's got to find that woman before Lou Stanton rips this town apart. Just don't take Mr. Polce in for questioning." Lucille may have sounded flippant, but her heart was pounding. If Matt didn't believe her, if he didn't buy her story...

"Fine. If Mr. Jacobs's story checks out, I won't question Mr. Polce. But if we haven't found Miss Stanton in twenty-four hours, I'm taking him in."

"Seventy-two. And Mr. Jacobs doesn't get interrogated either."

"Twenty-four and we won't question Jacobs."

"Forty-eight. Besides, tomorrow's Sunday. Do you really want to work on a Sunday?"

Matt growled. "Fine. Forty-eight. We will be back on Monday afternoon for Mr. Polce, whether it's his *wish* or not, and we will be coming with a warrant to search this house."

"Fine."

"Fine."

Matt turned to go. Lucille felt her body relax once he was no longer staring at her. Then he paused and looked back at her.

"I have one final condition."

Lucille's insides clenched again. Just like Matt to let her think she was home free and then lay in with a catch.

"You have dinner with me. Tonight. At my apartment."

It was Lucille's turn to growl. "You think I'll trade favors for sex?"

"Not sex, just dinner. I want to...talk to you." His voice was soft, and he wasn't looking at her.

The tone caught her more off guard than the suggestion. He sounded, she didn't know, broken, or something. Her heart beat a little faster, and not from nerves. "Okay."

"I'll text you the address. Eight p.m., okay?"

"Fine," she said one last time.

He kept his word and left, taking his policemen with him.

Lucille wandered back into the living room, feeling dazed and off balance. Brett was still perched on the edge of the leather couch like a scruffy but loyal guard dog, watching Michel as he rocked and moaned. For an artistic genius, Michel Polce was remarkably unhinged.

She walked to Michel's side of the couch and laid a hand on his shoulder. He looked up at her with those sad blue eyes. "The police are gone, Michel," she said in her most soothing voice. "They won't be bothering you." *For a while, anyway.*

"Thank you," he whispered.

"What'd you do? Give the detective a blow job?" Brett asked.

Lucille ignored him. "It's only temporary. Stanton pulled strings to get the investigation fast-tracked, and they can only hold him off for so long. If she doesn't turn up in the next forty-eight hours, I'm afraid they'll be back to question you."

Michel nodded. "Of course."

"You're both out of your fucking minds," Brett muttered.

Lucille's mouth twitched. "Do you have something to add, Mr. Jacobs? Or are you going to continue to be an ass?"

Brett stood. "Yeah, I do have something to add. I don't get how any of this concerns you. Why are you even here?"

"I am here because my client needs me."

"Uh huh. But why did you send the police away? It seems to me that with the attempted murdering and kidnapping, they are the very people who we actually need here, not you." Brett's face was red and angry.

Lucille's pulse raced again, and her lady business perked up and took notice. Matt had always told her it was weird how she got off on conflict. "If the police get involved," she said, talking down to him on purpose, "then Michel will be taken in for questioning. The media will get ahold of that, and the next thing you know, Michel's being framed as a kidnapper. Someone does a little digging and the murder attempts come up. It is my job, Brett, to see that none of that happens."

"Don't you think that Michel's life is a little more important than his reputation?" Brett spluttered back.

She watched his mouth, unable to stop thinking about kissing him. "It's not my place to judge. I leave that up to the client."

Brett was speechless for about ten seconds. "You leave it up to the client. You leave it up to the client?"

"As I said." *How can someone so naturally attractive be such a pig-headed mess?*

Brett just nodded like a bobblehead doll. "Even if the client is completely insane?"

Lucille shrugged. *Naturally attractive?* "Again, not my place to judge."

"Will the two of you shut up?" Michel bellowed from the couch.

Lucille turned to look at him in surprise, immediately turned off and back in her senses.

Michel was lying down, but he seemed more lucid than he had a minute before. "There's only one thing to be done."

They waited. Brett crossed his arms and looked skeptical. Lucille tapped her manicured nails against her skirt.

"We have to go after Sylvia." Michel said the words with such authority, such firmness, it was difficult to reconcile him with the broken shell that had inhabited the space not ten minutes ago.

"Oh? Do you know where the kidnappers might have taken her?" Lucille was being sarcastic but Michel didn't pick up on it.

"Perhaps. I have some ideas."

"Lord help us," Brett muttered and fell back on the couch.

Michel wasn't finished. "We just need to make a list of possible places and then, taking my jet of course, search them. We'll be gone in a few hours and back before Monday, my beloved Sylvia safe in my arms."

Lucille knew this was her stop. After fighting for Michel all day, she'd have to walk away at the eleventh hour. She didn't do the action; only dealt with the aftermath. She didn't go racing around looking for errant heiresses. But then she'd also never had a client of Michel's caliber. Seeing this job through to the end would mean she'd have enough business to last her the rest of her career, however short that may be.

She stared at the wall behind Michel's head, trying to formulate a response. The wall was a pale blue that stood at odds with the rest of the Spanish decor. *Walk away or stay.*

"Michel...we're not police," Brett said. "Or spies, bounty hunters, or cartels. We're artists. We don't go on the adventure, we make adventure films."

Michel wouldn't be dissuaded. "What if Sylvia isn't back in forty-eight hours? What if they hurt her? What if they...kill her?"

"Can I remind you that we're talking about the woman who has tried, not once, but six times to kill you?"

"I don't care. I love her. Please come with me. I have no one else to ask, and you are my oldest friend."

Lucille heard Brett's groan of defeat. "Only because I have nothing, and I mean absolutely nothing, to lose."

"Thank you." Michel leapt up and kissed Brett on both cheeks.

"Ugh, get off. Now you really owe me. Well, *Lucy*? How about it?"

Lucille looked at the two men staring at her, one with earnest pleading, the other wary mistrust. She swallowed. "I can't." It was a poor start. She went on. "I mean, this is way outside of my role as your spin doctor, Michel. I can cover up your absence and hold off the police, but I don't get personally involved."

Why did she sound apologetic? She never apologized to anyone for anything.

"I understand." Michel's face fell again.

Brett frowned at her. The muscles of his jaw worked, no doubt holding back the scathing accusations he longed to lay at her feet.

Lucille couldn't stay there anymore. She had work to do and the stupid dinner date with Matt. She couldn't stand to look at her heartbroken, desperate client or his angry, attractive friend any longer. "I have to go. Text me when you have a plan so I can cover for you."

"Of course." The words came from Michel. Brett still hadn't said a thing.

She picked up the purse she'd discarded on the chair and started out of the room. She stopped, met Brett's gaze, and said, "For God's sake, don't get yourselves killed."

She walked out of the mansion, her heels echoing too loudly on the stone floor.

# CHAPTER EIGHT

B rett waited for the front door to close before turning to Michel. "And why do we need her?"

Michel shot him a look. Brett waited.

Michel sighed. "Remember that rapper we were into like ten years ago? The one who turned out to be in all those cults?"

Brett nodded. "HiFli."

"Yeah. And you kept saying it was weird that he was so famous but no one knew about the cult thing? Everyone thought he was doing charity work instead?"

"That was Lucille?"

"That was her uncle. Simon Anton."

Brett whistled. "Impressive. So why didn't you contact him?"

Michel rubbed his hand over his face. His whole body was tense and on edge, his expression a dark shadow of frowns. "No one has seen Anton for eight years. Now, can we please focus on how we're going to find Sylvia?"

Brett opened his mouth to ask something else, but Michel glared at him and he closed it again. He still had so many questions. *Why has nobody seen this guy in eight years? Does that include Lucille? Is she her own uncle in disguise? The last thought is preposterous. Maybe. Good idea for a plot, though...* "I wonder what Lucille said to make Detective Adams go away," he said aloud.

"For fuck's sake, Brett! My fiancée is missing, probably being tortured, possibly dead." Michel choked on the last words.

A punch of guilt stopped Brett's thought train. He stood, shifting from foot to foot, while Michel sank into another wave of sobs. Then he did the only thing he could think of—he went to the summer kitchen and fixed them both a generous pour of whiskey.

"Here," he said, shoving the whiskey in Michel's face. "Drink this."

Michel took the glass without a fight and downed it in a few gulps. He gazed up at Brett through watery, angsty eyes. "Brett, you are such a good friend to me. After all I did to you. I know this is a rough time for you too, and I just...thank you for being here. I'm sorry—"

Brett slapped Michel across the face.

Michel blinked, his cheek turning red beneath his brown skin. "What was that for?" he asked, rubbing his jaw.

"Don't take this the wrong way, but you're a fuck-ing mess," Brett said, sitting in Lucille's vacated chair beside the couch. He took a long drink of his own whiskey. Why hadn't he thought to bring the bot-tle over? He remedied the situation and refilled Michel's glass, splashing more into his own for good measure. The day was shaping up to be a real fuck-ing shit show.

Michel gulped his whiskey. "I know. I mean, I can see it, I can see myself, but I just can't do anything to stop it."

Brett nodded. He could see himself drinking too much, sleeping with strangers he cared nothing for, wasting his life on a profession his family wanted, and failing spectacularly at it. No, there was noth-ing spectacular about his failing. It was a flailing, desperate failing that not even his dearest friends, of which he had none save the man next to him, wanted to hear about.

"What we need to do is find Sylvia, find out why she's been trying to kill you, and get this whole crazy situation cleared up."

Michel was silent for a few minutes. "I've been thinking. What if she actually does want me dead? What if it isn't a big misunderstanding after all?"

"Come on, Michel." Brett leaned over and slapped him on the back. "This is Sylvia we're talking about. My hot-headed cousin who loves you more than anything in the world. She probably got in with the wrong people, owes them money, and they put out a hit on your life. When they couldn't get you, they kidnapped her."

And, under the current circumstances, that theory sounded far more pleasant than the probable reality.

Michel took a deep breath. "You're right. Of course you're right. Sylvia loves me and I love her. We just need to talk it through and get things squared away with the kidnappers. Then everything can go back to normal."

"Yep, and whatever happens, Lucille will cover it all up so no one knows," Brett said. He meant it to be sarcastic. He still didn't get the point of Lucille, particularly now she'd run out on them when the going had got tough.

"I know."

Brett frowned. "Aren't you annoyed she ditched us?"

Michel shook his head. "No, she was right. This is way beyond her professional boundaries. Besides, she got the police off the case, which is already more than I thought possible."

They were quiet for a while, drinking. Brett's thoughts meandered back to how exactly Lucille had gotten the policemen to leave them alone. She had a history with the detective, that was obvious. She might have traded sexual favors. They'd certainly been gone for long enough. He didn't see Lucille Anton as the type of woman to get down on her knees, though. Especially on the stone floor in that short skirt of hers. No, she was the type of woman whose bribe would be allowing a guy to get her off, and that guy would be grateful for the opportunity. Brett knew he would be. The woman was sexy, particularly when she was angry. He would like to see her fall apart as she came, releasing all that pent-up tension in a moment of bliss that he'd administered.

He pushed away these fantasies. They'd only lead to heartbreak—his—and tears—again, his. "So," he said, breaking the silence, "you have some ideas

about where Sylvia is? And how we're going to res-
cue her from the kidnappers?"

"The first part, yes. It's likely she's been taken by
one of the Stanton's enemies." Michel blinked a few
times. "As for the second, I was hoping you would
know."

"Why would I know? If anything you'd know after
all that covert ops training you did for *Man Undercover*."

Michel shook his head. "Stunt double."

"All of it?"

Michel nodded glumly. "My face is worth too
much to risk doing my own action scenes."

"So we're fucked." Brett drained his glass. "More
whiskey?"

"Not much else we can do," Michel agreed.

Over the next hour and another bottle, they made
a list of all of Sylvia's possible enemies. It was long
and included everyone from the personal stylists
she'd fired to her sworn enemy, Reina Winter, to her
best friend, Ani Bennet, who she publicly bullied.
A few people they could cross off the list. Lucille
had had lunch with Reina that day, Brett had seen
her. Ani Bennet had been interviewed in the media
reports of the kidnapping. Everyone else, though,
was a strong possibility. They drank another bottle.

Next, they made a list of locations Sylvia might have been taken to. Turned out Michel did have ideas, lots of them. Over half the world was on their list.

Michel got antsier and drunker as the day went on. He was counting down the hours until Detective Adams returned to haul him off to jail, and counting up the hours since Sylvia had disappeared. It was obnoxious.

Brett excused himself to the bathroom. Michel's mansion had a his-and-hers bathroom set on the first floor. He'd always considered this weird. Weren't these supposed to be near the master bedroom so the couple didn't have to share? It had to cause confusion during parties. Not that Brett was ever invited to Michel's parties anymore. He wondered if Michel even had parties. Somehow he didn't think so.

He picked the "hers" side and headed straight for the medicine cabinet. Just as he'd suspected, it was jammed full of pill bottles, the prescriptions made out to Sylvia Stanton, the contents mostly intact. He grabbed one that seemed most similar to Valium and, when he went to refill the whiskey glasses, crushed it up and sprinkled it in Michel's drink. A few minutes later, Michel was passed out on the leather sofa, snoring.

"Awesome," Brett said to himself, and he went upstairs to look for clues. He rummaged through Sylvia's walk-in closet, checking for who knew what. *A gun? A letter that said she wanted Michel dead? A picture of her new lover? A death threat from possible kidnappers?*

Though knowing his cousin, there was a definite possibility that there weren't any kidnappers and she was playing them all. He could almost guarantee that, despite having a rich fiancé, Sylvia was in need of funds. Her dad had cut her off after all and there was some question of her being written out of his will.

*Thunk.*

He froze, listening over the sound of his pounding heart. All he could hear was Michel's snoring echoing off the cathedral ceiling. The house was still. But he'd definitely heard a sound—a thunk. It wasn't the house settling; new houses were made primarily out of concrete, and stone didn't settle.

Brett removed his shoes and snuck, barefoot, out of the bedroom, his breathing thundering in his ears. *Had Lucille come back? Or one of the servants? Or the kidnappers?*

Michel was helpless on the couch downstairs, knocked out with drugs and copious amounts of liquor. If the kidnappers did come back, they'd have an easy job of it. Michel would go without a struggle, and his blood would be on Brett's hands.

Brett ran then, straining to hear Michel's snoring over his adrenaline rush. At the marble staircase he didn't pause but catapulted down the steps. Only something had changed since he'd climbed those same stairs not half an hour prior. One of the stones was askew, but he didn't notice until his foot landed on it, his full body weight engaged in the forward velocity.

In a feat of desperate refusal to die at this precise moment in time, he grabbed the bannister as his feet slid out from under him. He flailed through the air and landed with a thud on his back as his right arm wrenched behind him, ripping his shoulder from its socket. The pain knocked the consciousness from him, and he missed the would-be murderer's exit.

# CHAPTER NINE

*F*orty *missed calls.* In the short time she'd been at the mansion, her phone, still on vibrate, had gone off forty times. Under other circumstances, she'd have berated herself for missing so many urgent messages. Under the current circumstances, she felt annoyed. As she pulled out of the tree-lined driveway, she also felt distinctly shitty.

*Walking away was the only option,* she told herself again. Going off on a hostage retrieval mission meant risking everything: her secrecy, her other clients, all that she worked to achieve.

*What sort of precedent would it set if I was willing to go to those lengths for a client? Next thing I know I'd be personally involved in all my cases.* Lucille shuddered.

It wasn't like she was breaking any agreement. In the mess of Sylvia's presumed kidnapping and her ex-boyfriend's ill-timed arrival, she hadn't given

Michel the contract. She worked for him in word only, and that she had no trouble breaking. She shouldn't even be writing him a press release without upfront payment and a nondisclosure agreement, but after seeing that hurt look on his face, not to mention the stunned betrayal from Brett, covering their tracks felt like the bare minimum of guilt appeasement.

Only Lucille wasn't supposed to feel guilt. She didn't do guilt. Still, her gut, the instinct she didn't listen to because of its stupid self-righteousness, piped up. It reminded her that she'd been waiting for something like this for years; eight years, to be exact. It reminded her of the resentment she'd held toward Simon when he'd left her his business, his mortgage, his mountain of problems. The young girl who'd wanted to experience something besides the dark underbelly of humanity but who'd had to accept her life for what it was. She dealt in that dark underbelly. She handled other people's problems, other people's ill-conceived adventures, other people's lives.

Her gut told her that an opportunity had just been thrown at her head and she'd blocked it. This was her chance, her adventure. It had everything she loved—scandal, secrets, and hot men.

Her car stopped at a red light, her blinker ticking, counting the seconds as the door of her call to adventure closed. Brett and Michel would be flying around in the Polce private jet, hunting down the bad guys. They would find Sylvia, tackle her kidnappers, get to the bottom of her murder attempts, and save the day. They would do it all without Lucille. They would get the credit and the glory, and she would manipulate the press so no one knew the whole story.

Then there was her life ahead. The empty house that was never home. The endless parties where no one knew who she was. James was the only person she'd consider calling a friend, and he worked for her. She had no friends, no family she knew how to contact, no home. Pathetic didn't begin to cover it.

Lucille's anger won out over despair. No. There was no way those men were leaving without her. No way she was going to subject herself to a future of loneliness and meaningless sex. Well, perhaps the meaningless sex. But she wanted friends, goddammit. She wanted parties where she knew people and they knew her. She wanted to go a whole day without dealing with a self-absorbed, drug-addicted celebrity.

Lucille was only a few miles from the mansion and hadn't met city traffic yet. She screeched her car into a dangerous, dramatic, illegal U-turn, pissing off everyone around her. Then her phone rang.

"If this is Christy-Anne," she muttered, swiping the screen. "Lucille Anton."

"Lucille, it's Reina." The model's signature purr was gone. Instead of a contented kitten, she sounded like a short-fused bomb with less than a minute to blow.

"Hello, darling. Look, this isn't a great moment to talk—"

"I've been trying to get ahold of you." Reina cut her off, her tone shorter.

"Was that you? I'm sorry, I've been dealing with some time-sensitive issues that—"

"I am not in the mood to be bullshitted, Lucille. Do you know who just visited me?"

Lucille thought it best not to guess.

"A detective. A detective, Lucille! I thought he'd found out about Andreas."

Lucille's stomach, only a heartbeat ago full of anticipation and excitement, plummeted.

"But no. He wanted to talk about that bitch, Sylvia. He knows about my history with her and thinks that I did something to her. But I didn't! I haven't seen her in months." Her voice rose, growing more desperate and hysterical.

Lucille swore.

Reina screeched, "What's going on, Lucille?"

In her most soothing voice, Lucille said, "Reina, I promise you, Detective Adams has nothing on you." She explained about Sylvia's kidnapping but didn't go into exactly how or why she was involved in the case. Even a famous supermodel didn't get to know everything. "I made a deal with Detective Adams that he would drop the case for the next forty-eight hours. Clearly he hasn't been keeping his end of the bargain."

Reina was silent for a moment. Then she said, in a slightly less belligerent tone, "I can't have the police sniffing around in my things."

"I know, and I am on my way to clear this up right now. I promise you, he won't find out about Andreas." It was a promise she shouldn't make and couldn't keep, but one didn't get by in the celebrity spin doctor world without lying to all of their clients, according to Simon Anton Rule #4.

"You had better."

"I'll call you tomorrow, okay? And we'll talk about your new collaboration with Igmar, all right?"

"Fine." Reina hung up.

Lucille scowled at her steering wheel and did another illegal U-turn. She wanted to smash something. The adventure was canceled, at least for her. By the time she got back to the Polce mansion, the boys would be long gone. She thought about throwing her phone out the window and running over it with the car. Then she'd leave all her responsibilities behind and skip town with a couple of nutcase artists.

How dare Matt go back on his word. Sure, she'd planned to stand him up but now it looked like she'd be showing up after all. But in no way would she be having dinner with him, the manipulative bastard.

She raced back to the city, her anger healing the sting of disappointment.

By the time she pulled up at the address Matt had texted her, Lucille was furious. She was more furious when she realized she was on time for their date. It would have been more satisfying if she'd made him wait for hours before showing up to eviscerate him. She sat in the car fuming, watching the minutes tick by and hoping her absence had him squirming.

They'd met the day she'd arrived at the mansion to live with Simon. Her mom's latest husband had died under mysterious circumstances. Lucille was pretty sure her mom was innocent, but she was also the prime suspect. Having just graduated college, she'd had nowhere else to go, so she ran, broke and in debt, to live with the man who'd been raising her her whole life. Her mom hadn't put up a fight—Lucille always went to Simon when things got bad. Lucille used to wonder why no one had bothered to ask her how she felt about the whole thing—first being sent for by her mother when she was stable enough to live in one place for longer than a few months, then back to the home she'd grown up in with Simon when it had all come crashing down. If they had asked, she'd have said she didn't mind. Simon had been the most stable family member she'd had. Plus, he was interesting, fashion savvy, and had promised to introduce her to his business when she was old enough, though she'd been fairly certain it was something illegal.

That first day she'd showed up again at his door, wearing her cutoffs, plaid button-down, and cowboy boots, her VW Bug filled with all her belongings, Simon had opened the door, taken one look at her, and said, "Honey, you know I love you and I'm so happy you get to live with me now, but that"—he'd looked her up and down—"is not coming in the house."

"This is what all the girls are wearing," she'd whined back.

"Maybe in podunk Kentucky—"

"Nashville."

"Whatever. But not here. This is Beverly Hills. Dress for it."

"Ha ha, hilarious. What're you gonna do? Make me change outside?"

He'd thought about it for way too long.

"Really?"

Simon had rolled his eyes and smiled. "Those boots are definitely not coming in."

Lucille—she'd been going by Lucy at the time—had grinned and gone to grab her bags. As she'd been hauling a huge suitcase out of the car, she'd caught the heel of said boot on a hole in the asphalt and stumbled, trying to catch her bag before it fell on the ground.

"Whoa," a voice behind her had said. It hadn't sounded like Simon, but it was hard to tell from a "whoa."

A hand had reached around and grabbed her arm, another hand holding onto the suitcase. She'd leaned into the hand and steadied herself, easing the wheeled bottom of the bag to the ground. Her eyes, following it down, had caught sight of a pair of black, masculine sneakers. The type of shoes Simon wouldn't be caught dead in. They'd been attached to a pair of muscular, tanned legs, baggy running shorts, a sweat-drenched t-shirt that showed off the broad chest and defined muscles beneath it, and a pair of large, muscular arms with big, warm hands. The guy had been a little taller than her and sweaty from his run. He'd had a striking, well-defined face without an excess ounce of fat anywhere. His dark hair had been floppy and fell into his eyes all the time. He'd been a twenty-two-year-old girl's wet dream, and she'd had a crush on him right from the beginning.

Of course, her boot had still been stuck and she'd nearly fallen over again.

"Whoa," he'd repeated, putting his hand around her arm.

She'd nearly died from the touch.

"Are you here visiting?" he'd asked, nodding at her stuff.

"Um, no. I'm moving in with my uncle."

The guy had smiled so broadly that she'd forgotten to breathe. "Great. Welcome. I'm Matt. I just live a few...miles away."

"Lucy," she'd managed. In her head she'd congratulated herself for getting her name right. Staring into his blue eyes, she'd decided to make a conquest of him. He was cute, he ran, and he helped out strange girls who were unloading their cars.

It had been great for a while. Toying with him, making him want her, playing games only she knew the rules to. But Matt had thought her a wholesome girl when he met her, and he'd been determined to make her one even after he found she wasn't. He refused to play her games and instead insisted on long talks in which he'd told her how he felt and she'd pretended to feel the same. He'd almost succeeded in taming her, as she'd come to think of it. Maybe he would have succeeded if he hadn't gotten Simon arrested and forced her to testify against him.

The apartment building was an ugly, modernist rectangle located down the block from the police station. She buzzed and he let her up. Once inside, she stalked up the stairs, cursing her love of high-heeled boots and old buildings with rickety steps. At his door, she knocked, loudly and repeatedly, until he unlocked it. She pushed past him, waited for him to close the door, and then whipped around, eyes narrowed and hands trembling.

Matt was wearing the t-shirt she'd gotten him for his twenty-eighth birthday, the black one with the Blues Brothers on it. His hair was messy and he needed a shave. He looked like he had eight years ago, but with more gray and deeper laugh lines.

Looking at him made Lucille's blood boil. If he'd worn that old shirt to endear himself to her, it wasn't working.

"Hi," he said, frowning.

"What right," she said, speaking slowly so each of her words would cut deep, "do you have to go around interrogating people?"

Matt frowned deeper. "Every. I'm a detective."

"Reina Winter isn't even involved in the case."

Matt went from confused to tense. "I beg to differ. She and Miss Stanton have a history of animosity. I wouldn't be doing my job if I didn't follow all possible leads."

"We made a deal."

"We made a deal that I wouldn't arrest Michel Polce for forty-eight hours. Not that I wouldn't question other potential suspects."

"Reina Winter did not kidnap Sylvia Stanton."

"And you know that for a fact?" Matt narrowed his eyes.

He could see into her. Through her. She knew he knew when she lied. "Yes, I do."

"And you're willing to testify to that?"

Those words were too much. They struck that trigger, the one that would always be there between them. Her testimony for Simon; her testimony against Matt. She gritted her teeth and pushed down her desire to punch him in his smug face. "Yes."

Matt broke eye contact. "Fine, then I'll leave Ms. Winter alone. Do you still like all your food to be separate from each other?"

Lucille didn't like how this had gone. She felt more angry words bubbling up. She wanted to scream at him for ruining her chances to experience life. Again. "We aren't done talking about this."

Matt looked up from where he was spearing shrimp onto a plate.

"You can't just come back into my life, screw things up, and pretend it isn't happening." Lucille felt angry tears prickle behind her eyes.

Matt set the plate down on the counter. "Lucy...I only came back into your life, as you call it, because I had to. Because it's my job to investigate crime.

Believe me, seeing you is as much of a shock for me as it is for you."

"Why the fuck are you wearing that shirt?"

Matt rubbed his neck, like he did when he was embarrassed.

Realization trickled down her back like a cold stream of water. The fire that drove her there was doused in an instant. "Matt. Why are you wearing that shirt?"

He didn't respond.

"You've been looking for me."

"Sort of. Not really. I didn't know you were still in town, until today." Matt looked at the wall over her shoulder.

"Why?"

"Are you going to yell at me again?"

"That depends. Why?"

Matt met her glare. He looked like a little boy being forced to fess up in front of the whole class. "When I saw you today it brought up some things. I never forgot you. And I hated the way things ended between us."

"You mean how you arrested my uncle and had me tried as an accomplice?" This was starting to feel like a bad romantic comedy, the kind she hated but always cried at anyway.

"I didn't know they'd go after you. I was trying to get you out of there. I felt terrible when they put you on trial."

"So you forced me into this date because you felt guilty?"

"Not exactly."

Lucille's annoyance was rising again. After the day she was having, she wouldn't need an Ambien to sleep. Her emotionally wrung-out body would probably crumble the minute she closed her front door.

"Then why *exactly* am I here, Matt?"

He was still watching her, his face blank and guarded. Instead of an answer, he crossed the space between them, grabbed her by the hips, and kissed her. His mouth was sweet and familiar, like the taste of a favorite childhood candy. She didn't want sweet and familiar. Sweet and familiar led to other things—to feelings, to memories, to love.

Lucille dropped her purse. She froze. She pushed him, hard. "Hang on."

"Sorry."

Lucille glared. If he thought this was going where she thought he thought it was going, he was right, sort of. If they had sex, he'd be more emotionally invested in it than she would be, but at the moment, in her anger, Lucille didn't care. Matt had screwed with her. It only seemed fair she return the favor.

He was going on about something. How he shouldn't have overstepped the boundaries and misread the moment and they could still eat their dinner as friends.

"Shut up," Lucille demanded. Before he could protest, she kissed him, reaching her arms around his back to explore his well-defined muscles beneath the tight-fitting t-shirt.

Matt broke away and searched her face.

Even as her heart pounded from the sexual energy between them, her jaw tightened, closing off any emotional reaction.

"Lucy—"

"Matt. If you say another word, this isn't going to happen." If he said he still loved her, it was over. It had to be over—she wasn't heartless. If he didn't say it, then she could pretend this was just what she wanted it to be: a hookup with an old boyfriend who meant nothing, who, in a few hours, she'd walk away from and never look back.

Matt closed his mouth and nodded. She looked at his lips, not wanting to read the message he was screaming to her through his eyes. Weren't cops supposed to be closed off from their emotions and married to their jobs? Why did she have to date the only one who had a good work/life balance and was in touch with his feelings?

Lucille gave Matt a push, causing him to stagger backward until he hit the front door. She stalked toward him, hoping he'd get the idea that gentle was not in play tonight. Grabbing the hem of his t-shirt, she pulled it off him. When he protested, she kissed him, biting down on his bottom lip. He got the message.

Matt grabbed her hips, turned them both, and pushed her up against the door. She slammed against the wood with as much force as he had. Before he could pause to apologize or ask her if she was okay, she wrapped her legs around his waist and yanked his head down to her chest, where her breasts were straining against the low neckline. Judging by the insistent pressure against her thighs, her breasts weren't the only things straining.

He nipped at her cleavage, then licked, pushing at her blouse. His right arm wrapped tighter around her, freeing the left up to ease the buttons apart, slowly, deliberately, and with all the time in the world.

Lucille groaned in frustration. *At this pace I am going to fall asleep before we get to the actual sex part.*

She ground her hips into him, pushing toward him with straightforward intent.

Matt looked up, his face flushed with arousal, youthful in his excitement, a contrast to the premature aging of his hair. "Bedroom?" he gasped.

Lucille considered. As fun as it was to be fucked up against the door, she had far less control in this position. During their relationship, when she was younger and newer to sex, she'd been more willing to experiment, but if she wanted to get off fast, this wasn't going to cut it.

She nodded and released her legs from around his waist. She let him take her hand and lead her down the hall to his very tidy bedroom with his very tidy department store comforter and flannel sheets. Telling him now that grown men sleeping on flannel sheets was sad would kill the mood, and at the moment, she was all about the mood. Instead, she gave him a long, hard look up and down his body and said, in a soft voice, "Strip."

Matt stiffened. His usual easy compliance was completely gone. When he stared at her, his eyes were guarded. "Lucy. I don't play those kinds of games anymore."

Lucille frowned. This was not how things were supposed to go. "What kinds of games?"

"I'm not going to lie down and be some sex toy that bends to your every whim. Maybe when I was in my twenties, but now I want more."

Lucille was stunned. *He'd known? More?*

Matt sat on the edge of the bed and reached out his hand to her. She stared at it. He set the hand back down in his lap and gazed at the suddenly fascinating hardwood floor. "I want to cook you dinner. I want to make love to you. Lucy—I've never stopped loving you."

The rage was back, swift and boiling. She ground her teeth and resisted the urge to growl. "Why did you have to say that? Why did you have to go and ruin everything?"

Matt's head snapped up. "Ruin everything? What was there to ruin besides your plan to control me?"

"I wasn't planning to control you."

"No? You didn't show up here with the intention of fucking me so hard I'd agree to stay away from your case?" Matt had to be angry now too. He didn't shout, though. He was too well trained for that. Instead, he spoke in a low, hurt voice that cut through all of Lucille's self-protective barriers.

"Does that even work?" Not a great comeback, but it was the first thing that had popped into her head.

"I don't know, Lucille, but that's never stopped you before, has it?"

"Uh uh, no you don't. Don't make this my fault. I'm not the one who broke us up. I'm the one whose family was torn apart, who had to stand trial against her own uncle because her boyfriend decided to get involved where he wasn't welcome."

"You have trust issues."

"No shit."

They stood in silence, both seething. Lucille knew she should storm out, but there were so many more things she wanted to scream at him. More about how he'd betrayed her, and some stuff about how he'd wanted them to be married and have kids and to put her in this neat little box while he went around shooting guns and living his dream.

Matt spoke first. "Did you ever love me?"

There was that tortured voice. The one that made her ache even as she wanted to strangle him. And the urge to strangle was winning over. "Goddammit, Matt, grow up."

She strolled out of the bedroom, picked her purse up off the floor, and was about to slam the door behind her when Matt spoke.

"Our deal's off. If you want to keep doing your little spin doctor thing, that's up to you. Just know you'll have the whole police force as your opponent."

# Chapter Ten

Brett heard someone call his name through the darkness. Why was everything so dark? It was the middle of the day. Or maybe it was night. Maybe he was sleeping one off. So why was someone shouting his name?

Cold water hit him square on the nose, dousing his whole face in frigid pain. He spluttered, got water in his mouth, and spent a few moments choking on that. He opened his eyes as he coughed and got water in them too. Finally, after several minutes of rapid blinking and strangled, hacking yelps, he cleared his face enough to look around him. He was lying on the floor of Michel's entryway, surrounded by a puddle of water. It was night, and Lucille Anton was standing over him with an empty glass and a stony expression.

"What the hell did you do that for?" he demanded.

She shrugged. "It worked, didn't it?"

"I nearly drowned! Didn't you see me choking?"

She rolled her eyes. "You are so goddamn dramatic. Where's Michel?"

Brett started, then clutched the back of his head, cringing when he felt the giant lump. "Isn't he on the couch in the living room?"

"I haven't checked there yet. I just walked in and found you unconscious."

"And you decided to throw cold water on me?"

"Uh, no. First I dragged you down the rest of the stairs. I figured it'd hurt less if you were still out."

"What happened?" Brett asked as his body, aching and throbbing, joined him in the conscious world. His right arm, in particular, was on fire and he couldn't move it.

Lucille eyed him. "I was hoping you would tell me that."

Brett rubbed his temple with the hand he could move. "I don't know. I was going through Sylvia's closet when I heard a noise. I walked down the stairs but slipped somehow...there was something wrong with the stairs...anyway, I think there's something wrong with my arm."

"I'd say so."

Brett turned his head. His right arm was stuck out to the side like a child's stick figure drawing where the shoulder isn't connected correctly to the torso. He turned away. "That can't be good."

"No. Especially since we can't exactly take you to a hospital right now." Lucille reached down, took his left arm, and pulled him to standing.

Her hands were strong and oddly comforting. Odd because Brett didn't think anything about the woman in front of him was comforting. "Why the hell not?"

"Super-secret, time-sensitive mission ring a bell?"

"Oh right, that. We haven't gotten very far on that."

"You've had the whole afternoon and evening! Michel said he some ideas about where she went. What do you mean you haven't gotten very far?"

Brett flinched. "Stop shouting. I probably have an untreated concussion."

Lucille made him follow her manicured forefinger with his eyes. No concussion.

"I tried to look for clues, you know, before being possibly murdered. But after I knocked Michel out, I didn't know where to look."

"You knocked Michel out."

"Yes."

"Michel. You knocked Michel...out."

"Right."

"Michel. As in the only person who knows what the next step is in this whole fucking mess? As in the person who's in danger of getting murdered at any moment? That Michel? You knocked him out and then went and got yourself nearly killed on the stairs?" Lucille's voice was quiet and scary and hot.

*So not the time to be turned on.* Still, it did distract from the pain. And the shame spiral brought on by her oh-so-sensible words. "He wouldn't shut up about Sylvia. It was that or kill him myself."

Lucille mumbled something and stalked down the hall, leaving Brett to get himself to his feet, one arm dangling worthless by his side. She was wearing different clothing. Instead of a skirt and blouse, she was in dark jeans and a white, lacy top over a black tank. Brett's brain wasn't up to going from observation to conclusion just yet, though. All it told him was she looked nice in the outfit; not necessarily approachable, but at least less like a stiletto-wearing ninja. Idea for his next movie, should he survive this: ninjas who fight in skirts and four-inch heels.

Lucille returned. "You are so lucky he's still there and hasn't been kidnapped by the murderers."

Brett poked his right shoulder. It hurt like hell. "Has he come to?"

"Not yet. Did you guys at least come up with a plan?"

"Um...no."

She sighed and looked around the room. Crossing to the side table, she sank into the ornate wooden chair beside it, her whole body collapsing into the wood. She rubbed her face, smearing some of her makeup. Brett bit his lip. *For the pain*, he told himself. *Only for the pain.*

"What?" she asked when she caught him watching.

"Nothing." He looked down at his bum arm. "I thought you were taking a backseat role in this whole recovering-the-kidnapped-fiancée business."

Was it his concussion or did Lucille look guilty?

"I was. But...we have a problem. Remember how I said Detective Adams was going to leave us alone for forty-eight hours?"

"Yeah."

"He's not."

Brett sat back down on the floor. There wasn't much point standing when all the blood was rushing around his body in a panic dance, charging from his throbbing arm to his head to other places.

"Well, that sucks." He wondered what had happened. Had one of her carefully laid plans blown up in her face? He didn't know her well enough to know if she had carefully laid plans. She just seemed like the type of person who would.

He lay down on the ground. It was cold and gritty and very, very hard. *Like my penis,* a thought told him. *What? No. That doesn't even make sense.*

The pain must be killing him.

"Hey. Are you okay?" The click of her heels reverberated around his head.

He grunted and opened his eyes to find Lucille standing over him, watching him with one raised eyebrow. Her expression landed somewhere between concern and disgust. He didn't need that right now. He closed his eyes again.

The heels clicked away across the floor. "There's gotta be some Vicodin somewhere in this place."

He heard her climb the stairs, each footfall growing farther away. The cold floor was comforting on his aching head. The silence of the night, unbroken by the sounds of traffic, ambulances, or gunshots, was soothing. He could imagine he wasn't lying on his old friend's foyer floor with a dislocated shoulder after someone who had been trying to murder said friend got him instead. Rather, he could imagine he was on a beach somewhere, the sand cool and soothing in the evening air. He'd walk the edge of the water, the white-tipped waves greeting him with each swell. He'd look for stones in the shallows the way he used to when he was a kid. His family would have left already, forgetting him behind like they always did, coming back hours later when they remembered about their son. In this time before they returned he could listen to the waves, feel the sand, and find the rocks. For once he could be at peace.

He heard his mother's voice, calling to him. He ran away, kicking up sand behind him, his footprints lost in the waves, but still her voice was there, always right behind him. He whirled to face her.

"Leave me alone, Mom!"

"I don't know what kind of delusion you're under, but I'm not your mother."

Brett opened his eyes. Lucille was standing over him again, this time looking angry. He opened his mouth to apologize but didn't get to say a word before she shoved two pills down his throat and poured water in after them. He choked and sputtered but was forced to swallow.

"What did you give me?"

"Vicodin."

"Oh." He was lying on the leather sofa where he'd left Michel. How had he gotten here? Michel's face came into view.

"I found a sling. I'm going to pop your shoulder back into place and then wrap it in that. This may hurt," Michel said in a lilting voice.

That woke Brett up. He tried to scramble away but put weight on his right arm by mistake and howled.

Michel was making soothing noises. "Shh, shh, it's going to be all right. Just lie back and relax."

"Relax? *Relax?* How can you tell me to relax?"

"Because if you don't, I can't set your shoulder properly."

"Exactly. Have you ever even set a shoulder, Michel?" Brett's voice was rising. He felt hysterical. From the look on Lucille's face, he must have sounded hysterical.

"Not in practice. But when I was doing research for *Yesterday's Child* I shadowed a doctor for a week and saw him set a number of dislocated bones."

"And I'm supposed to trust you? Because you saw somebody do something while researching a role?"

Michel looked him straight in the eye. For a man who'd himself been hysterical and then drugged not hours earlier, he was surprisingly calm. "Yes."

Brett looked at Lucille, pleading with her.

"Oh no, you do not want me setting your arm," she said.

That wasn't what he'd meant. He didn't want anyone but a real doctor touching his injury, but there was no real doctor, only Michel. With all the trepidation of a seasoned veteran going into battle, he held out his injured arm. Michel felt around Brett's shoulder, his hands warm and soothing. He placed one hand on either side of the joint, counted to three, and pushed the bone back into place.

The pain was excruciating. As he blacked out again, Brett wondered why they couldn't have waited until the Vicodin kicked in to do that and why he hadn't thought to ask.

"Now," Lucille said as Brett slumped into the couch, "back to business."

"Just a moment. I have to put the arm in the sling."

Lucille sat down in a nearby chair and watched as Michel lifted Brett's arm and slid it into the white cotton sling. Brett's head was thrown back on the couch, his hair falling over his closed eyes, his lips parted.

Brett was everything she avoided—a sloppy, funny drunk with major self-esteem issues. Michel was the type of man she went for—beautiful, well-dressed, rich, and famous, with an ego the size of his bank account. Or men like Matt—successful, distinguished, serious men who cared more about their career than her. Those were her type, not the adorable sleeping man on the couch who she'd seen pass out three times in the span of an hour. Yet here she was, attracted to him. An attraction that'd been brewing for longer than she'd like to admit.

She felt a strange pang of guilt about having said she hated his film. It was the only movie she'd watched all the way through in years. It had made her laugh. It had made her cry. The DVD sat beside her bed and had sparked a baby crush on its creator. A crush that had grown when she met the man in person. She'd never tell him any of that, of course. They'd find Sylvia—soon, given the recent evidence—and go their separate ways. That would be that.

Michel straightened and crossed to the opposite loveseat. "I thought you weren't going to get involved?"

Lucille had surprised Michel when he'd woken to find her dragging an unconscious Brett into the sitting room. He'd recovered and helped her heave his friend onto the vacant couch. The drugged sleep must have helped him immensely, because he was a powerhouse of energy in a way Lucille hadn't seen him since...ever. Although she'd only just met him the day before.

Lucille told him about the fuck up with Matt, heavily edited. Client boundaries and all that.

Michel frowned. "If the detective is on the case too, that means..."

"Michel," Lucille called him back. "It doesn't matter. When I was searching your medicine cabinets for Vicodin, I found this note on the counter." She picked up a piece of lavender stationary from the coffee table. It read,

*If you want to see her again, bring 20 million dollars to the symbol of Stanton extravagance.*

"It's from the kidnappers," Michel breathed. "But the symbol of Stanton extravagance?"

Lucille shrugged. "I was hoping you'd know."

Michel stood, pulled a list from his pocket, and began to read from it, pacing the room as he did. "Could it be...? Not the mansion. That's Sylvia's childhood home and the first place Lou Stanton would have checked. The Stanton office building is ostentatious but not extravagant. It's possible they mean one of the beach houses, but which one?"

Lucille turned the note over. "Oh wait, there's more. 'I'm on Mino Island, dummy,'" she read aloud. *Lovely girl, Sylvia.*

"Of course! The Stantons' private island! Why didn't I think of that before? If they were going to ransom her, of course they'd take her to the island." Michel went charging out of the room.

"Uh, Michel, what about the twenty million?" Lucille called after him.

"I'll have my accountant meet us at the jet with the money in half an hour."

"Right." *Celebrities,* Lucille thought. *Always running around in their private jets, handing out twenty million dollars like it's spare change. Getting kidnapped and owning islands. What a beautiful, fucked-up world this is.*

It was nearing four in the morning by the time they'd roused the accountant and tracked down the pilot, and Lucille had lost the argument about bringing Brett.

"Finally," Lucille grumbled as Michel boarded the plane, briefcase in hand. Staying up late was not her strong suit, and now she was up for a second night in a row with the longest, most draining day of her life in the middle.

Michel gave her a pained look but didn't respond.

No wonder people loved him so much. He had the tormented artist act down pat. That single look had held the anguish of his soul in it, mirrored in his gorgeous blue eyes.

It was a good thing he was paying her so much or she'd be at home, in bed, asleep.

*You wanted adventure, didn't you?* her mind pointed out. A few days ago she'd been going through the same old routine, all the while wanting to throw her phone out the window and take off. Well, here she was, on an adventure. But why did it have to be *this* adventure? Why did it have to involve saving one of the bitchiest women in the world, only to tell her to stop trying to kill her fiancé? *That is not the plot line of some terrible soap opera. That is my life.*

If Mino Island turned out to be one of those rustic camping-only places, she was turning around and going home. She felt a rising panic. She could still get off the plane.

"Please prepare for take-off." The pilot's voice crackled over the speakers.

*Dammit.*

Brett shifted in his seat behind her but didn't wake up.

Lucille had been resolutely against bringing Brett. He'd been unconscious for hours and had an injured arm. The kindest thing they could do for him was let him stay home and rest. But Michel insisted, saying that Brett would never forgive him if he were left behind. Lucille wondered whether Brett would say the same.

They needed to discuss the plan of action, if there was one, for when they landed. Lucille looked over at Michel, sitting across the aisle, wearing earplugs and snoring softly. They had time.

# CHAPTER ELEVEN

Brett jerked awake, jostling his arm and hissing through his teeth. It was dark wherever he was. Armrests. A chair in front of him. A little window with the shade pulled down. He was on a motherfucking plane. Of all the places he'd woken up after a bender, this one took the cake.

He looked down at his arm. Someone had put it in a sling. Maybe they'd taken him to the hospital after all. In his dream, though, he remembered Michel grabbing said arm while going on about research and then snapping the bone into place. No one had even offered him a drink for the pain. It must have been reality—in a dream, he would have at least gotten a morphine drip or a bottle of scotch.

The fact that he was on a plane had been established. The why and how and where-to remained mysteries. He peered around, the hazy glow of the emergency exits his only guide. It was night. Planes didn't turn off their lights during the day. *Well done, deductive reasoning.* It was night. On a plane. A private plane. Michel's private plane, he guessed, given there were only two other passengers and the one on his right was Michel.

Michel had his seat leaned all the way back and was wearing earplugs and an eye mask. He was snoring. Lucille, in the seat in front of Brett, also leaned back, but without the sleep gear. She snored even louder.

Brett stood up to get a better look around but realized, halfway there, that he hadn't been sitting at all; his seat was reclined as well. And he was wearing a seatbelt. He fell back with a smack and a groan that did nothing to interrupt the REM cycles of his fellow passengers. *No wonder the angles are all off.* He undid the seatbelt the way the flight attendants always showed him to and sat up. *Dizzy.* His head felt like it was floating around in another hemisphere but hadn't bothered to invite his body along. He swung his legs over the side and stood. *Wobbly, but functional.* He stumbled forward, grabbing the back of Lucille's seat. Then he turned and faced the prone figure of his best friend. Perhaps he should start saying former best friend and get used to that now.

The plane jerked and he fell backwards into Lucille's lap. Lucille woke up with a shriek, just as Brett covered her mouth with his uninjured hand. She glared at him and nipped his palm.

"That's not going to work on me, sweetheart. I have sisters," Brett said. He felt Lucille close her mouth, her lips barely touching him. He lowered his hand.

"Get off me," she growl-whispered.

"In a moment. I'm not very steady yet." Actually, he couldn't feel his legs. He knew they were there because he could see them, but they weren't responding to his brain. "Where are we?"

"You're really heavy. I can't feel my legs." Lucille gave him a push.

"Me neither. Scoot over, this is a huge seat." Brett nudged her to the right side and maneuvered his own body between her and the armrest, his left arm on top. They ended up half lying next to each other, with Brett's injured arm between them, like lovers in a hospital bed.

"Why am I doing this?" Lucille asked him.

"Because neither of our legs are working."

"Hmm. The feeling's coming back to mine."

Brett felt her move her legs experimentally. She grimaced at the sting of renewed circulation. His legs felt fine already but he wasn't going to mention that. Or move just yet.

"What the fuck were you doing?" she asked him. They were so close together he could feel her breath on his face when she talked.

"I was trying to punch Michel in the face."

Lucille nodded a little. "Any particular reason?"

"This time? For kidnapping me and putting me on a plane in the middle of the night. Plus, the whole me-nearly-getting-murdered-in-his-house thing."

Lucille nodded again.

Brett was on a roll. "Which, come to think of it—why was that stair loose? If Sylvia is the attempted murderess and she's been kidnapped, who was in the house tonight?"

They were silent for a little while, not looking at each other, both thinking.

"Mino Island," Lucille said finally, meeting his gaze.

"What?"

"That's where we're going. Mino Island."

With their eyes locked together and their faces so close, their lips were inches apart. Brett swore he heard a hitch in Lucille's breath and could hear her heart thudding in her chest. He could feel the heat of her body, not touching his but a hair's breadth away, smelling of some sort of floral perfume. He took advantage of the situation and kissed her.

It wasn't a graceful kiss—graceful didn't work in their awkward position—but Brett went all in. He lifted his head a little to push Lucille back into the chair. With his good arm wedged underneath him and his injured arm useless, only their mouths touched. Which was why, a second later, Brett was unable to catch himself when Lucille shoved him away so hard he fell to the floor with a thud.

Michel stirred in his sleep, opened his eyes, glared at Brett on the floor, and closed them again.

"What"—Lucille had sat up and was now also glaring at him—"was that?"

"Sorry," Brett mumbled, rubbing the hip he'd landed on. "Misread the moment."

"Not really." She still frowned, but it was softened, serious instead of angry.

It was Brett's turn to look confused. "Okay, what?"

"You didn't misread the situation. I've been thinking it would be beneficial for us to fuck. This sexual tension is only going to hold us back." It was like Lucille was teaching a class; her voice was clinical and devoid of emotion.

"Okay." Brett didn't know what else to say. He'd never been propositioned so dispassionately before.

Not that he'd been propositioned much. But still, he'd always thought that, when the time came, the woman would put a little more oomph into it.

"But not here. Sex on planes is awkward, gross, and probably won't work with your injury. We'll have to wait until we get to the island."

Brett nodded to his commanding officer. He wanted to salute but thought better of it. Lucille wouldn't appreciate his feeble humor. And she might rescind the sex offer. "Is there liquor on this plane?"

Lucille nodded. "Michel said there's a bar in the back."

"Good, that's good." Brett pulled his abused body off the floor. "Let's go get a drink."

It didn't take long for Brett to start feeling more like himself. His worries were momentarily silenced, his shoulder pain had softened to a dull throb, and he was having more fun than he'd had in a long time. Lucille Anton wasn't the stuck-up snob she pretended to be. She'd spent the last hour getting tipsy and telling him about the shit an anonymous past client had gotten into and expected her to clean up. Brett had never laughed so much in his life. His face hurt from smiling. He hadn't even asked for the story. It was like the alcohol or the sleep deprivation or the promise of sex or something had loosened the dam of Lucille's compartmentalized life and out had spilled this brilliant, self-deprecating comedy.

Brett reached over and poured them another glass of whiskey with his good arm. "What about this thing with that slutty pop star and the boy-band douchebag?"

Lucille arched an eyebrow at him. She was turned toward him, her elbow resting on the bar, her posture bent enough that he could see down her shirt just a bit, enough to see the crest of her breasts. If she'd been wearing that short dress she'd had at the launch, he'd be seeing a whole lot more. He tried not to feel disappointed and failed.

"You read *Celebrity Goss*?"

"What self-respecting failed celebrity doesn't?"

Lucille shook her head. "Naturally. That whole thing is such a fucking mess."

Brett gestured around him. "As opposed to the completely routine recon mission we're on now?"

"At least Sylvia Stanton is open about attempting to murder Michel."

Brett nodded. "And she did leave us that note telling us where she was, which was thoughtful of her."

"Christy-Anne and Ryan"—Lucille grimaced when she said their names—"on the other hand, are the most whiny, backstabbing, cheating, self-absorbed people I've ever met. And I've dealt with cults, eating disorders, and a whole range of sexual perversions. Those two are just..." She shivered in disgust.

"What's so bad about them? You know, so I can start emulating their behavior and become a teen pop star?"

Lucille laughed. "Yeah right, like you could ever pass for seventeen."

"Is that how old they are?"

"No. They're both twenty-eight. They just pretend to be younger for the media. Christy-Anne hasn't had a birthday in eleven years. Ryan just dyed the tips of his hair blond. If they ever actually had a child, I would not be the only one to call social services."

"The baby story is made up?"

"Yeah, that was me."

"What's really going on?"

Lucille shot him a look over the rim of her glass as she took another sip. "I can't tell you that."

"You told me about your other client."

"Anonymous past client. I can't tell you about a current client. What if you sell the story to someone?"

Brett gestured to himself. "Look at me. Am I the kind of guy who would seduce a woman with alcohol, convince her to tell me all her secrets, and then sell them to the press?"

"Yes."

"Touché."

They were silent for a while, an uncomfortable, twitchy sort of silence. Two almost-strangers sitting there at the bar. Brett wondered if Lucille was feeling like he was, that, though there was the promise of sex between them, he had a greater urge to spill all his family history, life woes, and plans of how he was going to turn it all around in the future. It was different than before, in the bars when he'd assailed fellow customers with sob stories. He felt warm and vulnerable, like he would bubble up if he didn't tell all his secrets right then and there. But he didn't want to bore her or chase her away. The woman next to him was successful, wealthy, and breathtaking, and he wanted to know everything there was to know about her. His own life was so small and empty in comparison, a life that could be written up in two paragraphs on the inside flap of a book jacket. Borderline alcoholic, fails at relationships, lives alone, doesn't talk to his family, and generally hates his life. It was depressing even in his head.

To chase the thoughts away, he asked, "So, how did you get into the celebrity spin doctor thing anyway?"

Lucille gave him a long frown. "You heard about my uncle, Simon Anton?"

Brett shrugged. "A little."

Lucille looked down at her glass. "He started the business years ago. Well, not that many years ago; he's actually not much older than I am. I started working with him after I graduated from college. Things were great for a while."

Brett waited for her to continue. "Then?"

"Then I don't know. A job went bad for Simon. I wasn't involved; he didn't want me to be. But I was there when the police came for him, and I had to testify in the trial and then learn about the news of his escape along with everyone else. He's on the run somewhere, I don't know where. He hasn't talked to me in eight years, just left me with his houses and his business and all his problems."

There was a bitter edge to her voice. Brett's heart ached for her. He reached his hand out to touch her, to rub her back and soothe her, if he could. *Would she accept the contact or would she throw it off?* His hand hovered, debating. Finally he settled on her arm, just lying there. Her skin shivered under his touch and he swallowed, his whole body buzzing.

But he kept his voice quiet, treading this unknown territory with exceptional care. "What about your parents?"

Lucille laughed, and it was ugly and bitter. "I have no idea who my father is. How cliché is that?" She stopped talking for a long minute. "And I don't talk to my mother."

She shrugged off Brett's hand. Brett drew back, stung. But he said, "I don't talk to my family either."

The look Lucille gave him had a second of pure, raw vulnerability. Then she was stoic once more, an untouchable beauty. She stared at him, and the corners of her mouth turned up a bit.

"What?" Brett's heart was in his throat. All throbbing that was not relegated to his pants or injured shoulder was bursting out of his chest.

"I can't help thinking my Uncle Simon wouldn't approve of you," she said with a real smile this time.

It was Brett's turn to frown. "Oh. Why not?"

She shook her head. "It's hard to explain. You'd have to meet Simon."

*It's the whiskey,* Brett's brain decided. He didn't have feelings for her, it was the whiskey. Of which he was still on his first glass, and that only half gone. The amount he'd drink when he wasn't drinking. "Do you care?"

Lucille arched an eyebrow at him, her whole face alive with mischief. "If he doesn't like you? Not really. I kind of like you."

"Dear God, why?"

"Because, Brett," she said, leaning in until her forehead rested against his, "you're just all out there, you know? You're like, 'I'm a mess.' You don't try to hide it."

Brett wanted to protest. He didn't want her to like him because he was a mess. He wanted her to like him because he was...

She was kissing him now and he couldn't, didn't want to, think.

They made out against the bar, a hard, passionate battle of warring sexual tensions. Lucille took charge, pushing him into the mahogany and kissing him fiercely. Brett didn't mind. With his sling, he couldn't do much grabbing or caressing. He did get his hand under her tank top and was inching it upwards when she stopped him by biting his lower lip, hard. He gasped and froze, like a naughty child caught stealing cookies from the jar.

She released his lip and put her mouth close to his ear. He was taller than her, but the way she had him pushed back, they were close to the same height.

"Later," she whispered. As she spoke, she slid one hand down to his straining jeans, resting there for a moment before turning and walking back to her seat for their landing.

Brett stood where he was, breathing and leaning against the wood for support. The woman was...sexy. The devil. An enigma. His personal hell and savior. There was a good chance he was more than a little bit in love with her.

# CHAPTER TWELVE

Lucille smirked as the plane began its descent. The trip was already turning out better than she'd expected. Brett barely made it to his seat before the pilot announced they were landing. He was turning out better than she'd expected, too. There wasn't any whining with Brett; no protestations of endless love or the need to know what she was thinking. He'd asked about her business and clients but hadn't pushed her about her family. Plus, he kissed like there was nothing else in the entire world he'd rather be doing.

Michel woke up as they roared to a stop. It was a stumbling group who exited the plane, crippled by sleep deprivation, injuries, and intoxication. A ragtag team the likes of which Disney wouldn't know what to do with.

When they set foot on the ground and there were no campgrounds, pack mules, or outhouses in sight,

Lucille exhaled. In fact, for a "primitive" island there was a hell of a lot of civilization.

"Michel, I thought you said Mino Island was rural."

Michel looked at her, his sleep-tousled hair shimmering sexily in the mid-morning light. "It is. There isn't a cultural scene at all, and the only theater company on the entire island has been doing variations on *Hamlet* for the past decade."

"I thought you meant we'd have to travel on horseback or be camping in the wilderness and cooking our own food." For all of her relief, Lucille felt strangely disappointed. But she hated camping and cooking, and the last time she'd ridden a horse had been when she was twelve, and she'd hated that too. Perhaps it was just indigestion.

Michel gave her a look. "If that were the case, I wouldn't expect any of us, least of all myself, to be here."

She turned to glance at Brett, who'd been standing behind them. He shrugged. "I guess true love has its limits." He said it quietly so Michel didn't hear him.

Lucille watched as the pilot unloaded Michel's enormous suitcase. "If you didn't pack for camping, what's in that bag?"

"Clothes."

"Just how long do you think we'll be here?"

Michel shrugged. "I intend to wait as long as it takes for Sylvia to come back to me. But that does not mean I have to wear the same outfit while doing it."

"Yeah, it takes a lot of hard work to look that devastated," Brett added.

Lucille bit her lip so she didn't scream. She wanted to remind them that Matt and the police department were hot on their trail, not to mention that, unlike the unemployed celebrities, she had a job to get back to. Just as she was gearing up for a long speech about responsibilities and meetings, Brett whispered in her ear, "Look on the bright side. With Michel occupied with his appearance, we'll have plenty of time to get to know each other."

When she turned to glare at him he gave her a wicked grin.

The island was gorgeous. A small piece of land off the coast of New Zealand, only ten miles in diameter. What served as an airport was a paved strip of ground, home to only one small two-seater and now Michel's private jet. The bulk of the island, the part that wasn't white sandy beaches and swaying palm trees, housed the Stanton Resort, a huge luxury hotel so exclusive Lucille had never known it existed. It was modeled after a Greek island, with white stone walls, cobbled paths, and wrought-iron railings. The atmosphere was one of exaggerated calm and obscene wealth. The perfumed air spoke of lavish floral arrangements and aromatherapy spa packages. The few guests around in the late morning were dressed in white, flowing clothing over tiny fabric-swatch swimwear. It took Lucille about ten seconds to decide she loathed the place.

It was the kind of place her clients went to when they wanted to hide, to leave their troubles for her to clean up. The type of place where no one ever got billed because they would never notice the money leaving their bank account. It was the type of place she used to dream of going to, of belonging to. Anyone could belong here, if they paid the right price.

A man wearing a three-piece suit, despite the eighty degree weather, met their white limo and welcomed Michel personally. Apparently, Michel had a suite there. Apparently, his friends were automatically given adjoining suites. Apparently, they didn't need to check in or worry about the bill; it was all taken care of.

"I think I'm going to be sick," Brett muttered after Michel and the man walked away.

"Too much whiskey?"

"Too much freesia."

After they'd settled into their suites, they reconvened in Michel's sitting room.

"Which room is Sylvia staying in?" Lucille asked, tapping notes on her tablet.

Michel was already wearing a Speedo and nothing else. "Hmm...I forgot to ask."

Lucille tried to exchange a look with Brett, but he was busy pouring himself a drink at the bar. His grimace indicated his arm was still hurting. And no wonder. They hadn't gotten him to a hospital to have it checked out.

Lucille wondered about what it would be like to have sex with a man with a dislocated shoulder. He'd probably be weak and vulnerable, easy to flip on his back and have her way with. She shivered at the thought. Or at the air conditioning that came on at that moment and cold-showered her.

Back to the fuck-up at hand. "What do you mean you forgot to ask? How do you forget to ask?"

Michel looked cranky. "I don't know. It probably had something to do with the fact I've had a very emotional few days. Not to mention being drugged by my supposed best friend yesterday." It was Michel's turn to shoot a glare at Brett.

Brett shrugged and poured another drink.

Lucille frowned at Michel. "Did you insist on bringing Brett along so you could keep an eye on him?"

"Keep your enemies close."

"Hey," Brett protested. "You don't honestly think that I had something to do with Sylvia's kidnapping."

Michel sat in one of the sitting area armchairs, his abs rippling on the descent. "No. But it is fucking annoying being roofied by your best friend."

Brett snorted. "It was for your own good."

Lucille relaxed and started typing again. For a minute she'd thought Michel actually suspected Brett but no, just the men being flippant in the face of danger. Again.

"Whatever." Lucille cut him off. "We don't have time to deal with the rift in your bromance. There is a homicidal heiress who needs rescuing somewhere on this island, and I, for one, am going to go ask the desk staff if they know anything about it."

But she never made it down to the front desk. She didn't even make it out of the suite. The next moment Lucille found herself hurled across the room. Time slowed down, but her body wasn't responding. She saw the floor coming toward her, felt the heat on her side, smelled the tang of burning hotel furniture, and couldn't do a thing about it. Her only thought as she fell was, *What the shit?*

In another moment, it was all over. Lucille was still awake and alive, but covered with a layer of plaster and ash. She coughed and pushed the debris off of herself. The soot would never come out of her clothes. *There goes a perfectly good outfit.*

Nearby, more debris was moving. Michel spluttered to the surface, his mostly naked body covered in small scrapes. Lucille couldn't help thinking his change into the Speedo had been a bit preemptive, considering. Still, she needed to make sure he wasn't injured. He was her client, after all. But she couldn't pick herself off the floor just yet.

"Michel, you're bleeding."

"What?" Michel shouted, squinting at her through the unsettled dust.

She motioned to his chest.

Michel looked down at his sculpted abs and the tiny rivulets of blood running down them. He pulled a splinter out of one of the scrapes. "Ah. Hmm. What happened?"

"The room exploded." Lucille's ears still vibrated in the aftermath of the blast. She shook her head. It didn't help.

"What happened?" Michel shouted again.

Lucille shook her head, this time at him. "The room. That room"—as she pointed to the direction the blast came from, she frowned—"Brett's room, exploded."

"I can see that."

"Then why did you…? Oh never mind." Lucille gave up when Michel cupped his ears and frowned at her. The next moment, though, it was she who shouted at him. "Where is Brett?"

Their eyes met in a mirror of panic. They scanned the sitting area, finding Brett against the wall beside the bar, still clutching his broken glass of whiskey, awake and moaning in pain.

"Brett! Are you hurt?" Michel pushed the remaining debris from his body and stumbled over to this friend, kneeling beside him so that Lucille had a front-row view of his ass. She tried and failed not to look.

"No more than I was," Brett said, his teeth grinding together. "What the hell happened?"

"Someone blew up your room," Michel said, running his hands over Brett's body.

"Dude. What are you doing?"

"Checking you for injuries."

Brett looked at him. "I will say this again. You are not a doctor. Nor do I want you touching me when you're only wearing a man thong. Understood?"

Michel rolled his eyes. "You are a terrible patient. Fine, have Lucille chcck you."

Lucille met Brett's eyes. He raised his eyebrow at her.

"As much as you might enjoy that, we need to figure out how Sylvia got a bomb in here," Lucille said. She still hadn't stood up. She didn't think she was injured; all her limbs certainly had feeling, bruised and battered feeling, but feeling nonetheless. And yet, for all the levity of Michel's life-or-death situation, this had been a close call. A very close call. If she thought about it too much, she'd realize how a few feet and the wrong room were all that had stood between her and death.

Brett nodded slightly, looking around at the remains of the bar, the shattered bottles, the liquor dripping to the floor. Lucille followed his gaze, feeling his pain. If she had to be a walking bruise, at least she wanted to be a drunk one.

Michel appeared to think for a moment, still kneeling like a bloody, Speedo-clad imitation of *The*

*Thinker.* "I don't think Sylvia did this. It isn't her style."

Lucille and Brett stared at Michel.

"So what, now there are multiple people trying to kill you? Who the fuck else wants to kill you?" Brett broke the smoldering silence.

"No, think about it. Sylvia's other murder attempts were all at our house, out of sight, quiet. Not explosive."

Lucille nodded. "True. So I don't think we should rule out the idea that someone else was trying to kill you."

Michel stood, looking very much like a centurion statue after the fall of Rome. "I don't think they were trying to kill me at all. I think they were actually trying to kill Brett."

Her attention turned to Brett, who was still in deep consideration of the bar. "What?"

"Who did you piss off? An ex-girlfriend? Wife? Stalker? Super fan?"

Brett's scowl deepened. "No one."

Michel, still talking to Lucille, added, "I don't think Brett has any super fans or stalkers. Certainly no girlfriends he was with long enough for them to want to kill him."

Brett clearly didn't like this recap of his life. He slid his leg out and kicked Michel in the kneecap as hard as he could in his current position. Which, judging by Michel's lack of reaction, was not hard.

Lucille rolled her eyes at them. "I, for one, would rather discuss this when we aren't sitting in the middle of a bombed-out hotel room. I need a drink, and since Michel's bar just blew up—"

The hotel manager who'd greeted their limo burst through the destroyed door. He stopped when he saw them and sighed, grasping at his heart in relief. "You are okay. You are alive."

It wasn't hard to tell he was talking only to Michel.

"Not really," Brett said unhelpfully.

Lucille waved at him to be quiet. "We're fine. But we have some questions for you."

The man shook his head. "They'll have to wait. Everyone must evacuate immediately. Take the stairs and stand away from the hotel until we give word."

Lucille shook her head. "We're not going to do that. And you are going to answer our questions. Now."

Someone laid a hand on her arm. She thought it was Brett and went to throw him off when Michel spoke.

"I think we'll all feel better when we've changed and calmed down."

Lucille bristled but kept quiet.

"But sir! It's not safe in here. I must insist—"

"Then we'll move to the other room," Lucille said. "Mr. Polce is not going outside covered in dirt and blood, and neither are the rest of us."

"We'll be in the lobby in ten minutes. Then you'll answer our questions," Michel added.

The man shut his mouth, nodded, and left.

No one moved or said anything right away, the shock of the bomb still overwhelming.

"I think I need a Band-Aid," Michel said finally.

Lucille, annoyed Michel had sent away the person they needed to interrogate, glanced at him. Sure enough, Michel's scratches were still bleeding. "I don't think one Band-Aid is going to cut it. Let's get you cleaned up and changed."

Brett cleared his throat.

They turned to him, sitting on the floor with his injured arm and dirty, soot-covered body.

"I'd really like to change too, but someone just blew up my clothes."

Michel walked over and pulled Brett to his feet. "You can borrow mine."

Lucille smirked when she caught sight of Brett's alarmed face.

# Chapter Thirteen

In theory, Brett and Michel were the same size. Only Michel was taller, broader, and way more muscular. And, apart from the current Speedo exception, exclusively wore suits. Brett grimaced at the closet of them, already pressed and hung in rows of subtly changing hues. He scowled down at his jeans and t-shirt. They would have been dirty but acceptable, torn from his fall down the stairs the day before but only at the knee. But then Michel had bled all over them while he was playing doctor, again. They'd have to go.

Then there was the problem of the arm. It hurt when he lifted it. It hurt when he didn't. He could write a fucking rhyme about all the ways it hurt. There was no way he could get out of his shirt without assistance. Assistance Michel couldn't provide while he was covering himself with Band-Aids. Brett didn't like his other option. Not because he didn't want her to see him naked; he did. But there were so many important, crucial things they had to deal with right now, and he didn't think his libido could handle another booty call near-miss.

His eyes scanned the bedroom, hoping to find another solution or that another person would magically appear. The room, with its breezy resort furniture, remained shiny, spotless, and empty. *Aren't bellhops and valets supposed to magically appear when you need them? What kind of five-star establishment is this?*

He sighed. At least he could change his pants on his own. No way in hell was he having Lucille zip up his fly unless there was some hanky panky involved first.

*Hanky panky? Who even says that anymore?*

He got the pants on, using his free hand to pull up one side and then the other, all the while trying not to get the blood from his shirt on them. By the time he was done, he was winded. From putting on pants. Things had really gone downhill lately.

He picked up the crisp, white button-down shirt—no way was he wearing a jacket in this heat—and headed down the hall to the room on the far side of Michel's. The hallway was deserted, evacuated after the blast. In the space that had once been his suite, there was smoke and the sound of a fire crew putting out the last of the flames. He could see lumps of blackened furniture, now soggy and dilapidated nearly beyond recognition.

The bomb had taken out his entire suite, the sitting area wall of Michel's suite, and the bedroom wall to the room on the other side. Brett wondered what the people in that room had thought or if maybe, horribly, they'd been hurt in the explosion. Who would do such a thing? Not only that, but who gets the room number wrong? Thank God they had or he wouldn't be standing there, half alive in a bloody shirt. But seriously. First the stairs and now the hotel. The murderers were losing their game. And where the hell was Sylvia? Wouldn't she want to be present when her fiancé-killing plot finally succeeded? Or maybe his earlier suspicion was wrong and Sylvia actually had been kidnapped.

Brett rubbed his head. Too many questions on not enough sleep, whiskey, or pain meds. He turned away from the wreckage and knocked on Lucille's door instead.

She opened the door at once, as though expecting him. She'd changed, replacing her business suit get-up with a sleek white dress that wrapped around her neck at the top, pushing her breasts in and up. Her hair was pulled back in a messy sort of bun and she wore some excessively strappy sandals on her feet. She was applying sunscreen.

"You're putting on sunscreen," Brett said, standing in the hallway in his bloody t-shirt and suit pants.

Lucille shrugged. "If you can't beat 'em, join 'em. I figure I'll get more out of the guests if I blended in. As opposed to dressing like whatever you're supposed to be."

Brett winced. "Michel only brought suits."

"And the Speedo."

"Yeah." He winced again and looked suspiciously at her. "And the Speedo."

Yep, she'd noticed his ripped, swimsuit model friend. If she was expecting anything of the sort from him, his chances of getting laid would plummet to nothing. Damn Michel and his stupid Italian good looks and confidence in his sexuality.

"So, what do you want? We have to be down in the lobby in a few minutes."

Brett shifted. This situation kept getting worse and worse. Now he wasn't worried about them having sex right now, lost in the throes of passion brought on by his naked chest. No, now he was worried this would ruin their chances of banging at all. He wasn't fat, but he didn't have rippling muscles either. "Right. So. I can't put on my shirt with this sling, and Michel is still Band-Aiding himself and hopefully getting dressed. Who knows how long that will take, so can you help me change my shirt?"

Lucille raised an eyebrow. He saw her swallow, and it made his heart leap a little. Something else twitched, too; something he was hoping would take no notice of the situation and stay where it was in his pants.

"Sure, come on in." Lucille stepped aside. She spoke in a clipped tone, not seductive, but not un-affected either.

Brett walked into the hotel room, identical to Michel's and what his used to look like. Lucille closed the door and turned to stand in front of him. She took the clean shirt out of his hand and laid it on the back of a chair.

"Are you right handed?" Her fingers closed around the hem of his t-shirt and tugged upwards.

Brett swallowed, his throat blocked by his pounding heart. "Yes," he croaked. "Why?"

Lucille's eyes were on the shirt she was pushing up over his stomach, slowly and purposefully re-vealing skin. When he replied, she looked pained, but her eyes didn't leave their hungry pursuit. "I was just wondering about whether you could write, and I guess you can't."

Brett's breath sped up.

Lucille reached up and unbuckled the sling from around his neck, holding one hand under his arm while she detached it from its white cloth casing.

"Good thing I've got terrible writer's block." Brett meant to say it in a light, joking tone, but he wasn't capable of jocularity at the moment. That he was able to speak at all proved miracles exist.

Lucille didn't react to his comment. She slid his arms out of the t-shirt, first his good one and then, even more gently than she'd removed the sling, his injured side. T-shirt freed, she folded it and placed it on the back of the chair, picking up the white shirt as she did so. This time she started with the bad arm, easing it through the sleeve, guiding his fingers through with hers. She moved behind him to pull the shirt around and put the left sleeve on. Shifting to stand in front of him again, she buttoned the shirt, top to bottom, her fingers resting on his hot skin as they pulled the sides of fabric together. Last, she replaced the sling, adjusting it so it went around the collar and not into his neck. When it was done, she stood back and eyed him up and down, a smirk on her lips.

Brett exhaled, releasing the air he'd been holding for the past minute. There hadn't been any gropage; no untoward touching of any kind. So why did he feel like they'd just had sex when all she'd done was put on a shirt?

If he had two good arms, he would push her up against the wall right then and take her there, standing up. If she wanted to, of course.

"You guys are not the same size," Lucille said. She turned away, picked up her purse from the side table, and swaggered out of the room, the smirk still dancing on her lips.

Brett crumbled where he stood. The control that woman had was unbelievably sexy. She knew he was in the palm of her hand, knew she'd left him on the edge and walked away, knew she could take what she wanted from him but didn't. He revised his earlier fantasy. If he had two good arms, he'd let her tie them to the bed and ride him all day long.

Had he really thought that? He wasn't into bondage. It must be the ocean breeze fucking with his brain. That or the pain and sobriety.

"Lucille Anton, you temptress, you minx, you siren." No, if he had two good arms, he knew what would happen. He'd be up all night writing horrible love poetry while she was off fucking Michel.

The thought had the cold-shower effect. Brett shook himself and caught up with Lucille and Michel at the elevator. They headed down to the main floor, where the rest of the hotel had also gone.

The tiled floor of the lobby was littered with irate guests, half-packed luggage, and stressed hotel staff. Brett and Lucille scanned the area for Sylvia or suspicious-looking people who could be kidnappers. It was tough. Everyone looked suspicious, half-clothed and scared, demanding increased security, early checkouts, transportation to the airport, or a new room away from the bombed floor. There was no sign of his cousin and no one who fit his stereotypical image of a kidnapper, bomber, or attempted murderer: a big man with an eye patch and a creepy leer.

Michel left and returned, dragging behind him the harried manager who was still shouting orders to his staff and encouragement to his clientele. When they reached Lucille and Brett, the man gave a long-suffering sigh and motioned them through the employee-only entrance.

Once they were in the man's spotless, windowless office, he offered them seats in the smooth, hard plastic chairs and insisted on bringing them coffee.

He pulled his chair around the desk and, with another longer-suffering look, sat down before them.

No one spoke during this exchange. Brett shot a glance at his fellow recon party members. Michel looked annoyed. Lucille like she was trying not to laugh.

"Forgive my rudeness earlier. I found myself quite out of my depth. Let me assure you, please, that this...incident will be looked into most thoroughly. If I find that one or more of my staff were involved in such an atrocious act, they will be arrested at once," the manager said, his face contrite.

"Never mind that. We think we know who did it," Michel said with exasperation. The explosion or all the blood loss must have snapped something to attention in his brain, because he was all business.

"You do?" the man squeaked. He was sweating, his receding hairline glittering in the overhead lights.

Michel dismissed the question. "Is Sylvia Stanton staying here at the moment?"

The man sat back. "I'm sorry, sir. I cannot give out the names of our guests."

Michel leaned forward, his face dangerous. "It is, and I mean this quite literally, and I'm certain you'll believe me considering one bomb has already gone off today, a matter of life or death. So I think you will find you can."

The man cowered in his chair. Michel didn't even have to touch a hair on his head. It must have been why he got so many offers. He was alarmingly good at persuasion when he wasn't out of his mind.

"Miss Stanton was here, but she checked out this morning," the man squeaked.

Brett wasn't surprised by the news. The bomb meant she or her kidnappers—the existence of whom remained questionable—knew they were going to be there. So it made perfect sense the perps hadn't waited around to be caught. Michel, judging by his reaction, didn't agree.

"She was here? She was here and you let her leave?"

The manager looked confused. "It is not our policy, sir, to detain guests who wish to leave. Particularly the owner's family members."

"But she didn't leave! She's been kidnapped!"

"Oh. Oh I see." The man repeated that a few more times.

Lucille stepped in. "Was there anyone with Miss Stanton?"

The man shook his head. "No."

"Anyone seen going in or out of her room? Anyone with her at any point in her stay?" Lucille's voice was calm. She'd even laid a hand on Michel's knee. To comfort him? Hold him back? Tell him she'd be there for him even if Sylvia ran off with another man or died or lost her looks?

Brett felt something. The only word he could think of was 'icky.' He felt icky, and it wasn't going away.

"Well...but no. It's only housekeeper gossip."

"Tell us anyway," Lucille said.

The manager looked more uncomfortable than he had before, if that were possible. He fidgeted in his chair, and his eyes circled the room, looking for an escape. "One of the housekeepers saw a couple of gentlemen going into Miss Stanton's room last night. A few minutes later they were joined by a third gentleman."

Michel leaned forward and asked menacingly, "And did the housekeeper see them leave?"

"We do not spy on our hotel guests." At this point the man was going to have a heart attack before the conversation was over.

"Really?" Brett cut in. "Then what about those security cameras all over the lobby and hallways?"

He was full of shit. He hadn't seen any security cameras, just assumed there were some. Luckily, he turned out to be right.

The man turned an even deeper red. "Yes, well, I suppose I could have the security team check those."

"We would be forever grateful," Lucille said with a little seductive smile.

Was she really flirting with the manager right now? With Michel, not to mention himself, right there in the same room?

"And, if it wouldn't be too much trouble, while you're at it, would you see if the person who blew up Mr. Jacobs's room was also caught on tape?"

The manager smiled back, nervous and twitching. "Of course."

"Thank you so much. It's a relief to find a man who's committed to the safety and needs of his guests."

The man blushed more. He was almost purple at this point, all from Lucille's flirting. Brett wanted to hurl. He stood up.

"If there's nothing else to do right now, I'm going to go lie down," he announced with more fortitude than he felt. What he really wanted to do was punch someone, the hotel manager if possible. "And I will need a new room, since mine has been blown up."

The manager blinked a few times as he was released from Lucille's spell. He jumped to his feet. "Right away. There are a, ahem, number of rooms that opened up on your floor after the...incident. Let me find one for you."

They followed the man back out to the lobby, got Brett's new keys to the room on the other side of Lucille's, and headed back up to their floor. Michel trailed behind, lost in thoughts that no one cared to ask him about.

Away from the crowd, Lucille spoke. "That was a waste, apart from confirming that Sylvia was actually was here. Let's hope those security tapes turn up something useful."

Brett couldn't stop himself from saying, "You were laying it on a bit thick, don't you think?"

She turned to him, her eyebrows raised. "It worked, didn't it?"

"Hmph."

She narrowed her eyes and smiled a little. "Are you jealous, Brett?"

He scowled. "No. But you can't just...change a guy's shirt and then go flirt with another man in front of him."

"Can't I?"

The elevator reached their floor. Lucille walked out first, leaving Brett to think of something, anything, to come back with. He grabbed Michel, followed her out into the hall, and stopped.

Lucille stood a few steps away from the elevator doors, frozen. Her face was stony and expressionless, her hands in fists at her sides. She had her eyes fixed on something. Or someone.

A man stood in the demolished doorway of Brett's former room, also frozen. A tallish man with styled blond hair and thick-rimmed black glasses. A man in a gray suit with a pink shirt and gray tie. A man who looked sort of but not exactly like Lucille.

# CHAPTER FOURTEEN

There was a rushing sound like someone had turned on all the faucets at once. Everything got quiet, and from a long way away she heard Brett's voice ask Michel if he knew the man, then ask Lucille if she was all right. He asked what was going on. Michel groaned again and told Brett he'd had enough of this shit for one morning and he was going to lie by the pool. The elevator dinged. The man moved toward her. She unfroze.

"Stay away from me," she said, backing down the hall.

"Lucy," the man, the specter, said.

"Don't call me that."

"Lucy," it said again. He said again. Ghosts weren't real. He was real.

She ran into something and heard a grunt. *Dammit, Brett!* He was standing behind her, blocking her escape. "Move," she told him.

"Not until you tell me what's going on," Brett, the asshole, said.

"Stop being a dick and get out of the way." It didn't work.

"Oh right, because we weren't in the middle of anything."

The man in the hall, the one who looked like Simon but couldn't be him, said, "I think, officer, you should listen to my niece and stay the fuck out."

It was a very Simon thing to say. The exact thing he would say in this situation. But Simon was away, somewhere far away in exile, never to return to the States again. Only they weren't in the States. They were on an island, a resort island for the rich and famous. An island so private the only people who knew about it were the guests. It was exactly the place Simon would be. "Simon?" she croaked, her throat constricting.

"Of course, Lucy. Who the fuck else did you think it was?" he said.

"This man is your uncle?" Brett asked. He was still standing right behind her. Not touching her, but close enough that she could feel his presence. It was comforting. Supportive.

Simon glared over her shoulder at Brett. "You know, for a detective, you're not very astute."

"I'm not a detective."

"No? Than what or who are you and why the hell are you here with Michel Polce and my niece?" Simon's expression hardened. He'd never liked to involve additional people in any of his cases. Lucille could see his gaze flick between them, probably wondering if she'd sunk so low as to bring along a fuck buddy. As if she hadn't learned from that mistake.

"This is Brett Jacobs. Michel's best friend. I didn't have a choice about bringing him, and neither did he. He's just a failed screenwriter Michel insisted we drag along."

"Hey."

Lucille shot him a look over her shoulder. He shrugged back, agreeing that it was true.

"Brett Jacobs. I saw your film, *Night Before the Apocalypse*. Hated it. It was decidedly awful."

"That's the general reaction," Brett said with a sigh.

"But um..." Simon glanced between them. "This is awkward."

Lucille realized what was going on but didn't want to believe it. Why did all the men in her life insist on being such psychopaths? "You blew up Brett's room, didn't you?"

He looked sheepish. "I thought you'd brought along another detective, Lucy. What was I supposed to do?"

Brett started toward Simon. "You could have killed me!"

Lucille put an arm out to hold Brett back. She didn't know why. Some residual family loyalty that hopefully wouldn't hang around for long.

"Aren't you glad I didn't?"

Lucille shook her head. "I need a drink." She grabbed Brett's good arm and tugged him toward her hotel room. "You two are coming with me. We have things to discuss."

Once they were behind closed doors, a round of drinks served—Brett lying on the couch, his injured arm cradled in his lap and his whiskey cradled in his hand, and Simon seated, cross legged and poised in a chair—Lucille glared at her uncle. Her uncle who was ignoring her and watching Brett, who, in turn, was giving him a death stare but was, for once, keeping his mouth shut.

"Are you sure you aren't a cop?" Simon asked.

Brett snorted.

"He's way too apathetic to be a cop," Lucille said for him.

"Hey."

Lucille shot Brett a glare. He shrugged and took another drink.

"Hmm. This is odd company you're keeping, Lucy. A client and a..." Simon trailed off, still looking at Brett.

"You don't get to judge. You"—she paused until her uncle met her eyes—"need to start talking. What the fuck are you doing here? Why the fuck did you try to blow up Brett's hotel room? And where the fuck have you been for the past eight years?"

Simon sighed and set his drink down on the coffee table, after first finding a coaster for it.

"Lucy—"

"No. You can't Lucy your way out of this. Answer me." The last part came out pleading. She was pleading, as much as she hated it. She felt like her twenty-two-year-old self, the young woman whose only stable family member had just been arrested and fled, abandoning her in the big old house with his business and no idea how to run it. Not to mention heartbroken from simultaneously losing the man she loved.

Simon sat back. His face was grim, all suave charm gone. He was watching her like he was seeing her for the first time. She supposed he was. Seeing that she wasn't the little girl he could distract with jokes and stories. She was older now, wiser, and sick of the bullshit she'd grown up in.

"I blew up the hotel room because I thought you had brought a detective to hunt me," Simon said.

"Do you really think I'd do that?" Lucille asked.

Brett shifted, the couch squeaking in protest. They both glared at him.

"Um, I'll just be by the pool," he said, grabbing the whiskey bottle and retreating from the awkward family situation.

As Brett exited, Lucille studied her uncle. He'd grown older during the years away. It was hidden beneath a dark tan and numerous face lifts, but she could see the age in his gray-speckled hair and the way he carried himself. Less arrogant. More weary of the world.

"I don't know, Lucy. When I left, you hated me. Remember? You told me you hated me, and I thought it was for the best. I hoped that hate would go away over time, but when I saw you arrive with Mr. Polce and who I thought was a detective, I thought I was wrong and it had grown instead."

Lucille sat down on Brett's abandoned couch. "I don't hate you. Even when I said I did, I didn't. I was mad at you for leaving me behind."

Simon reached out and grasped her hand. She let him hold it but didn't grasp his back. It was all too new, too sudden. It was barely two hours since she'd been almost killed in an explosion set off by the man next to her.

"Lucy, I never wanted to leave you behind. If I could've taken you with me, I would've. But…"

She raised an eyebrow at him. "But what?"

"Well. The truth is, that man wouldn't have let you go. I could see it from the way he watched you. He'd have followed you and me to the ends of the earth. There would be no rest for the wicked."

Lucille snorted. "While I'm sure that was true then, I very much doubt he would have followed me after what happened later that day."

Simon cracked a smile at her. "What did you do?"

"Just told his mother he was impotent and would never be giving her grandchildren."

Simon laughed at that. "That's my heartless bitch."

The tension had eased. Lucille still wanted to know why he was there but decided to let it slide for the moment. She'd missed him. Simon had been the only person she could talk to about work, about her absent, dysfunctional family, about her terrible choices in men. Because he had the same job, the same horrible family, and the same disastrous taste in men. Because he'd raised her since she was little, protected her, and cared for her, even when he was arrested and on the run from the law. Because he was almost fifteen years younger than her mom and only a few years older than herself—he'd been a kid raising another kid, and she couldn't help but love him for that.

So instead of an interrogation, they talked. Simon told her about his adventures around the world. About the scrapes he'd gotten into and the beautiful men who'd gotten him out only to leave him, broken hearted, for other beautiful men. He shared some of his fabled advice—don't date underwear models, they aren't always as gay as they seem. Being a celebrity spin doctor is not actual espionage. Don't get involved in actual espionage.

*Too late*, Lucille thought on that one. She didn't tell him why they were there, not yet. She loved her uncle, but it was his own rule, Simon Anton Rule #5: never trust anyone with a case, particularly your own family. It was about protecting the people you love first and foremost. She still didn't know the details of his arrest because knowing would have made her vulnerable and, as the twenty-something starting out in the business, she hadn't had the same friends in high places that Simon did.

Lucille told him about her clients. She updated him on the clients he'd passed along to her. She didn't mention Christy-Anne and Ryan. Judging by the nonstop texts she was still getting, there was no telling which case would end up in murder, Michel's or theirs. She recounted the details of her breakup with Matt and his reappearance the previous day. She skipped the part the near booty call the night before.

Finally, the laughter died down and the room grew tense again. They both knew what topic was up next. Lucille cleared her throat and asked, "Have you talked to my mom?"

Simon shook his head. "No, not really."

"Not really?"

He looked pained. "She tracked me down once, found an old phone number I was still using at the time. But she didn't ask about you. She just wanted money."

Lucille nodded.

"I'm sorry."

"Me too."

The door flew open and Michel, a refreshed and intent Michel, strolled in. "All right, talk," he said to Simon without so much as a who-the-hell-are-you. He didn't look surprised to see them talking. Lucille assumed that was because Brett had caught up to Michel and filled him in. Though with Michel, who knew.

"Excuse me?"

"The security tapes are back and you're on them. Specifically, you were the last man to go into my fiancée's room the other night. So talk."

Simon stalled. "Right. Well, it's not what you think. I mean, I didn't have sex with her or anything."

"That's not what I thought."

"Oh. Good. Because I didn't." It was a tactic Simon used when he knew something and didn't know who to trust yet. He got them worked up about something else and slowly steered the conversation away.

"Nice try." Lucille snorted. "But I know your tricks. Do you know where Sylvia Stanton is?"

Simon studied her, annoyed. "Fine. Yes. She's–"

Brett interrupted by running into the room, his hair stuck up everywhere, the too-big suit looking ridiculous on his slim frame. "The police and your ex-boyfriend the dickhead are here," he gasped.

Michel continued glaring at Simon. "Oh yeah, and the police are here. So talk fast."

Lucille glanced at her uncle. His face was expressionless, stony and hiding everything. *He's gonna run*, she thought. *He's gonna run and we won't get any answers out of him.*

He met her eyes, his still blank.

She shook her head slowly at him, which she hoped he understood to mean, *Don't even think about doing what you're thinking about doing. I will kill you.*

He looked back at Michel. "I know where Sylvia is and I know what the kidnapper's plan is. But the only way I can tell you is if we get out of here now. Because if those cops and my niece's dickhead ex-boyfriend find me here, you can bet they'll lock me up before you can say squat."

Michel glared at him for a few more moments and then relented. "Where do you suggest we go?"

"You have a private jet, don't you? That seems like a good start."

"What about Sylvia?"

Simon sighed. "With all the racket you made coming here, do you really think her kidnappers stuck around to be found out? They're gone."

Brett cleared his throat. "Um, so the lobby is full of cops and the hotel surrounded. Just how do you think we're going to get to said private jet?"

Lucille's brain had been working while they argued. There was an emergency stair exit she'd noted at the end of the hall. No doubt it led up as well as down. There had to be roof access and, given the luxury of the resort, a helicopter landing pad.

"Michel, does this island have a hospital?" she asked.

"No. Everyone is flown to New Zealand for medical treatment," Michel replied, frowning at her.

Lucille nodded.

Simon turned to her, his eyes gleaming with the same idea she had. "That would work."

"I know."

"Where?" he asked.

"The end of the hall, last left. You take Michel and have him call on the way. I'll take Brett," she said.

"Don't get caught," Simon said with a grin.

Lucille grinned back. The two men were watching them with confused, uncertain expressions.

"Do we still need the ransom money?" Michel asked.

"You brought the twenty million?" Simon said. His surprise was there and gone in an instant, so quick Lucille was sure Brett and Michel missed it. He shrugged. "Might was well grab it since you brought it all this way."

Something, besides the kidnapping, explosion, and murder attempts, was going on. Simon knew about it, and as soon as they were safely on the jet, Lucille was getting some answers.

Simon sprang into action, grabbing Michel by his muscular bicep and leading him out into the hall. Lucille grabbed Brett's hand and dragged him toward the elevators.

"What are we doing? Aren't we supposed to be running away from the police?"

The elevator dinged. The doors opened. Lucille pushed Brett inside. "I'm so sorry about this," she whispered. Then she kissed him.

# Chapter Fifteen

Brett didn't know what the hell she was sorry about, but he didn't mind the kissing. Her mouth was firm and sweet, her body hot against his, the little dress an inconsequential barrier. Her hands slid over him, pushing on his chest, gently forcing him against the back wall of the elevator. He wrapped his good arm around her, trying to pull her in, to feel all of her against him, but she put up a hand between them. Which was good and right for some reasons he couldn't remember. Maybe it had something to do with being in an elevator. No, that was okay. He was going to live in this elevator with Lucille forever, his hand on the small of her back, his mouth crushed against hers, the heat between them overpowering.

Their new elevator home dinged to announce a floor. Lucille pulled back as a pain shot through Brett's injured arm. He shouted, unable to help himself, and looked down at it. Somehow, without him noticing, no doubt because of all the kissing, she'd unbuckled the sling and then pushed hard on his newly relocated shoulder, popping it out again. His vision blurred.

Brett felt her arm around his waist, holding him up, walking him out of the elevator. In the hall, she let him slide to the floor. Her face appeared above his, a little blurry, but he thought she looked contrite. Served her right. People couldn't go around re-dislocating other people's shoulders, especially while making out with that other person.

Lucille leaned forward and gave him a quick kiss. "I'm sorry," she said again, and this time he knew what it was for.

Brett's thoughts were a jumbled mess. What if that apology wasn't for the shoulder? What if she was going to, he didn't know, pop out his other arm? Was she giving him a kiss for each injury she inflicted on him? If so, how come the first kiss was so great and this one so lame? He deserved another full make-out if she was, in fact, going to further mutilate him.

A man came into view, wearing a suit jacket and the name of the hotel. It wasn't the guy from before. He leaned in so close Brett thought the man was going to kiss him too. Instead, he asked Brett incomprehensible questions and then told him something about a helicopter and a hospital. Brett needed a hospital. He wasn't sure how the helicopter played into it, but if it led to a hospital, fine by him.

Then he was being lifted by more men and laid on a cot. Either they were taking him to get help or wheeling him to a corner to die. He didn't care which at the moment, as long as the pain stopped.

The cot moved, back onto the elevator. As they were sliding it through the doors, one of the men slipped and the cot careened into the wall, knocking Brett's arm against the metal. He yelled as the arm twisted and pain seared through his shoulder. He heard a barrage of apologies, but the whole place was already going dark.

There wasn't room on the elevator for her. Lucille hadn't counted on that. She'd found a staff member who wasn't the manager and didn't know Brett already had the injured arm. She'd made a big fit about him slipping on the lip of the elevator because it wasn't even with the floor. She'd made sure they knew she was prepared to sue if Brett didn't get flown to the nearest hospital for emergency care at once. And she'd done it all quietly enough on the second floor of the hotel that the policemen in the lobby hadn't shown up. But she hadn't realized there wouldn't be enough room for her on the elevator. She wasn't an architect and she had no sense of spatial dimensions, or how big a gurney was, or that they'd have four people to lift him onto it and wheel him, or that the man who'd come to help would want to personally escort the guest to the medical helicopter on the roof.

She hit the up button a few more times for good measure. The other elevator went down past her to the lobby and then came back up. The doors opened and Matt stepped out of them.

"Lucy." He looked genuinely surprised to see her. "What are you doing here?"

"I could ask you the same." Her heart sank, then pounded with anxious adrenaline. She needed to get off this island and far, far away from the man in front of her. The elevator left without her.

"I heard there was a disturbance on this floor and came to see if it might be related to the earlier incident. But no, just a hotel guest tripping and threatening to sue. Did you see anything?"

Lucille shook her head. "No. I walked up just as you arrived."

Lying to Matt used to be difficult for her. She found it much easier now that she hated him.

"That's unfortunate. You'd be a good witness." He didn't look like he was joking. His eyes were dark and his face solemn. "I don't suppose you were here earlier when the bomb went off?"

"I was here. I mean, not here here. I was by the pool, but I heard it. Did anyone get hurt?"

"No. Are you here with Michel Polce?"

"Of course I'm here with Michel. Think I'd be hanging around on a resort island halfway around the world if I wasn't?"

"Then you heard Miss Stanton was reportedly here."

Lucille spoke without a trace of sarcasm. "No, we decided to take a break from all that, do a little sun-tanning."

Matt's mouth thinned. "Cut the bullshit, Lucille."

"I'm not the one asking dumb questions," she said. She was getting more annoyed with each passing second. The helicopter would be there by now and they'd be waiting on her. Or they'd already left.

"Look, I'm sorry about last night. I mean, I'm not sorry about finding you again, but I am sorry for the things I said. I can't do this anymore. You, me, always fighting."

She narrowed her eyes at him. "Okay."

"We could give it all up, you know. Leave all these lies and secrets and betrayals behind. We could start fresh somewhere and be open and honest with each other. What do you say?" His voice cracked on the last part. His body language pleaded sincerity. It would take a cold, heartless bitch to walk away from a man like that, a man offering her the world.

But it wasn't the world she wanted, and right now she was more concerned about the man whose shoulder she'd dislocated hating her than the one in front of her. She hit the "up" button. The doors opened. "I have to go." It was all she could think to say.

As the doors closed, Matt gave her the saddest, most lovesick puppy face she'd ever seen in her life and said, "When you stop running, Lucille, I'll be there. And I'll still love you."

*Oh God. Oh God, oh God, oh God,* she thought as the elevator climbed to the roof. *Oh God. Also, what the shit?* What was she supposed to do with that? Drop all her life's work and run away to be Mrs. Matt Adams in a cute little house somewhere in a safe neighborhood where people only saw celebrities on

TV? *Things change, Matt. Things change and people change, not always for the better.*

She didn't know what Matt was playing at, but it wasn't going to work. She wasn't little bad-girl Lucy anymore. She was something entirely new. A woman with a heart of ice and the sex drive of a bitch in heat.

Speaking of which, the slowest elevator in the universe finally arrived at its destination, and she rushed to make sure her would-be fuck buddy was still good to go.

The helicopter idled on the roof. There was, luckily, room for all of them. Simon and Michel were already on board and pretending to be Brett's distant but concerned cousins. Lucille jumped on as Brett's wife, and the whole crew took off from the top of the hotel, heading across the short gap of ocean to where Michel's private jet waited to take them home.

The ride back was surprisingly uncomplicated, considering the cast of characters and the modes of transportation. Brett woke up when they got to New Zealand and was more miffed than the helicopter pilot when they told him they weren't actually taking him to a hospital but were flying back to the States on Michel's jet. Michel offered to set his shoulder again and, since they definitely couldn't see a real doctor with a fugitive in tow, Lucille had no choice but to let him, much to Brett's consternation. Luckily, Brett passed out again when Michel jerked his bone back into place, which stopped him from yelling about kidnapping and needing medical care. Michel paid off everyone at the airport and threatened the ones who continued to argue. They got on the plane, Brett lying back in his chair in a drug-induced daze, and turned their attention to Simon.

"Talk," Michel snapped. Throughout the trip, he'd been glaring at Simon, giving him threatening gestures when he thought Lucille wasn't looking.

She didn't care. Her uncle probably deserved it and much worse, especially if he knew where Sylvia Stanton was hiding and didn't tell them.

"Why were you in my fiancée's room?"

Lucille sipped her martini, letting the liquor burn down her throat. *When all this is over, I'm going to sleep for three days. Fucking psychopathic celebrities.*

Simon met Michel's glare, his face calm. "I was having a perfectly relaxing exile on the island when her associates approached me and asked for my help."

Michel frowned. So did Lucille. The more things unraveled, the less sense it all made.

"Why did she need your help?"

Simon took a long drink of his martini and answered solemnly. "To escape. She'd gotten away from her kidnappers and had hired some of the local men to be her bodyguards. She was terrified the kidnappers were onto her and needed to get off the island as quickly as possible. I had a sort of, uh, reputation around the place as being someone who's handy in tight situations. So I agreed, of course. One doesn't say no to a Stanton."

Michel's frown eased. He looked pained. "She was in trouble? But didn't she know I was coming? Why didn't she wait for me?"

Simon reached out and patted Michel's leg. They were seated at the bar, Lucille on the other side of Michel, where he couldn't see her face. Her frown only deepened, but she kept her mouth shut.

"My dear Michel, she wanted to wait for you, believe me, she did. She was sobbing, poor thing, about how she thought she'd never see you again. But when she was captured, she overheard the kidnappers say they'd only wanted the ransom as a ploy to get you there. They were going to kill you on sight."

Michel's whole face drained of color. His shoulders slumped, and Lucille held out a hand in case he was inclined to faint off his stool. The last thing they needed was another unconscious celebrity. Brett was work enough.

"She was protecting me," Michel whispered. "All this time I thought she was trying to murder me, she was protecting me from the people who were."

Simon's hand went from patting to rubbing Michel's muscular thigh. "She was. She's been your faithful lover this entire time. She wouldn't let any harm come to you."

"But...who wants me dead?" Michel looked up. He glanced back at Lucille, who quickly rearranged her face to an expression of contrite concern.

"Do you have any enemies, Michel? Anyone who's been jealous of your fame or your career? Perhaps an ex-girlfriend who you wronged or who went crazy when you broke it off?" Simon was in his element, playing therapist and detective to the stars.

Michel shook his head. "I don't know. I can't think of anyone. I mean, I had lovers before Sylvia, but I always treated them well. I know people are jealous of me, but last I knew all my stalkers had been arrested."

"Hmm," Simon said, his brow furrowed. Not too deeply. As he'd always told his niece, even fake frowns cause permanent lines. "We will have to get to the bottom of this. But you see why I can't take you to Sylvia, right? Not until we know who's behind all this and have had them apprehended?"

Michel nodded. "Is she safe, though?"

"Of course, perfectly safe. Which she won't be if you go after her. Now, why don't you get some sleep? It's a long trip, and we'll have a lot of work to do when we get back."

Michel nodded again and then looked up to meet Simon's eyes. "You'll help?"

"Of course. Lucy and I will do everything in our power to keep you and Miss Stanton safe."

Michel turned on his bar stool so he could take both of their hands. "Thank you. I don't know what I've done to deserve such loyal friends." Then he slumped back to his seat and was asleep in minutes, hiccuping pathetically.

Lucille slid to Michel's empty seat and hissed at her uncle, who'd gone, unflustered, back to his drink. "There are so many holes in that shitty story, I don't even know where to begin."

Her uncle looked at her over his glass, raising an eyebrow. "Don't frown, Lucy, it creates lines."

She scowled. "Don't treat me like a kid. I've been doing your job since you left. I know your tricks. About ten percent of that bullshit you just fed him was true. So why were you really in Sylvia Stanton's room that night?"

Simon stared at her for a long time, but she didn't look away, not like she would have when she was younger. He sighed. "Sylvia Stanton's henchmen threatened me when I was having a lovely day by the pool with this hot young guy, minding my own business. Don't even ask who he is, I won't tell you."

"I don't care who—"

"Okay, I'll tell you. He's the CEO of a well-known tech company. Quiet, nerdy, skilled with the sunblock, and gay as a rainbow."

She didn't have a response. Except to deepen her glare. It was his favorite tactic, distraction. "Get on with it."

"Whatever, don't listen to the interesting parts. Anyway, I had to meet Sylvia in her room later that night or else she'd have me outed and arrested there on the spot. So, I went to her room."

"And?"

Simon took a sip of his martini, swishing it annoyingly around his mouth before swallowing. "She wasn't kidnapped."

"Tell me something I don't know. Did she do it for the ransom money?"

He nodded.

"Because her father cut her off."

Simon nodded again. "She wasn't big on the details, but that's what I picked up. Anyway, she wanted me to blow up the hotel room of the supposed policeman who was coming with Michel. I was supposed to blow up your hotel room too, but I refused."

Lucille took the news of her attempted murder rather well. With all of the "accidents" going around, it seemed like only a matter of time before she was the victim of one herself. "Sylvia thought I was a cop?"

"No, she knows who you are, just like she knew exactly who I was. We have a mole."

Lucille almost laughed out loud but stopped herself before she did and risked waking up the sleeping travelers. "We have a two-person operation. If we had a mole, it would have to be one of us."

"I was giving you the benefit of the doubt. Honestly, Lucy, how could you get so sloppy?"

Lucille set her glass down hard on the bar. "Excuse me? I've been sloppy? I'm not the one who got fucking arrested."

"That was..." Simon shook his head. "Let's put all that on the back burner for now. Our top priority right now is to figure out where Sylvia Stanton is and how we're going to stop her from killing Michel Polce."

Lucille clenched her jaw. She stood up from the bar. "No. What we really need to do is get some sleep. I am exhausted. I have been dealing with deranged fiancées, ex-boyfriends, and you for the past forty-eight hours. I am going to sleep until I cannot sleep anymore, and then maybe, just maybe, I'll help."

Simon took another sip. "I didn't take you for a quitter, Lucy."

"No, no, no," she said. "You don't get to put that on me. I was hired to keep this whole thing out of the press, and that is what I intend to do. If you want to get more involved, that's fine. But I'm out."

Simon nodded. "You know there's a good chance I could be arrested on sight the moment I set foot in the country."

"That is your own damn problem. Good night."

Lucille choked back her worry. She was concerned about Simon getting arrested, about Michel being killed, about Sylvia Stanton trying to have her killed, about Matt showing up, about Brett never forgiving her for dislocating his shoulder. Again. She was worried about all of it. But she was also exhausted, jet-lagged, and desperately in need of a shower and her own bed. All of this mess would still be there when she got up. It wasn't going anywhere. *Except if your uncle gets hauled off to jail,* a voice in her head whispered. No, she told it, *he's too smart to let that happen.* He could take care of himself, just like he'd left her to do for the last eight years. She'd wanted adventure, but right now she wanted sleep even more.

She checked her phone. Forty-eight unread emails. One hundred and twelve missed calls. Three hundred and sixty-four text messages. Every single one of them from Christy-fucking-Anne.

# Chapter Sixteen

"What the literal fuck, L.?"

Lucille leaned back in her chair, rubbing her eyes. She may have slept for fourteen hours straight but it in no way had prepared her to deal with this. "Hey, Christy-Anne."

"Why the fuck haven't you called me? Didn't you get my texts?"

Lucille bit back her snarky reply about being fired numerous times in the Christy-Anne textual onslaught because, really, she just didn't want to deal with it. After walking away from Michel's case last night, she'd gone home and crashed, hard. Now, in the proverbial cold light of this air-conditioned rental, she felt unhinged. She was angry—angry at herself for getting into the mess, angry that she still felt an obligation toward Michel when they didn't even have a contract, angry that Simon hadn't called to find out why she'd bailed.

"Yes, I got your messages. All 364 of them. I just got home and was already dialing your number into my phone."

"I don't believe you."

She coughed back a snort and actually coughed instead. "Since you have me on the phone now, why don't you tell me what this is about?"

There was a lot of background noise on Christy-Anne's end. It sounded like she'd put silverware in a blender and set it on high. Knowing her, that wasn't an unlikely option.

"Where are you, and for God's sake, what's that noise?" Lucille asked, rubbing her temples and holding the phone six inches from her ear.

"Oh that? That loud, grinding racket that won't stop?" Christy-Anne was shouting, and not entirely for Lucille's benefit. "Ryan has decided to try some fucking DIY. The asshole is destroying my house, Lucille. He just drilled through a fucking wall."

Christy-Anne's voice was so sarcastic and venomous, Lucille couldn't hold back her laughter. She pressed her hand over her mouth, swallowing furiously so it wouldn't come bubbling up. Ryan was doing DIY. She could picture it—his spiky, gelled, highlighted hair clashing with the plaid shirt and tight denim he'd no doubt adopted, a power drill in one hand and a beer in the other. With that petite, slim body and the little bit of muscle that he could barely hang on to, it was a wonder he hadn't sent himself to the hospital.

Once she'd calmed down enough, Lucille tried to think of a solution, turning back and forth in her chair considering the options. Nothing came to her, so she stalled. "Why's he still there? I thought I read that you two had ended things for good?"

"Yeah, well, no thanks to you. You're supposed to be dealing with this shit. Instead I had to break up with him. On my own. And now the bastard won't leave. He says he likes it here! And that we'd make a good couple if we ever put all that pop star shit behind us. We would not make a good couple, L. And what pop star shit? I was so mad at him I locked myself in my room. But then he decided to impress me with some fucking home improvement and started drilling fucking holes in my fucking wall!"

Lucille wanted to know what Ryan could possibly be building. A bedroom bar? No, a fold-out massage table? Or a shrine to Christy-Anne? Now was not the time to ask. However, the conversation was turning out to be exactly what she needed after the intensity of the past few days. She found herself wishing she could tell Brett all about it, to cheer him up after the whole twice-dislocated-shoulder thing. But he probably wasn't speaking to her either.

Lucille got her silent giggles under control and tried to fake indignation. "That's terrible! But at least he's trying. And really, as your publicist, I shouldn't get involved in your relationship. It sounds like this is between the two of you."

"What the fuck do I pay you for? You're the one who brought him here, and then you weren't even here when I had to break up with him. You'd better make him leave. God, I'm so beyond furious I can't fucking talk to you right now."

"There's no need to be angry, Christy-Anne. Sure, we've had our rough patches this past week, but look at what we accomplished. No one knows about the affair with Marcus, you've had cover features in all the national magazines, and you can't tell me that every single minute with Ryan has been horrible. You dated him for five years, for God's sake. Some of that must still be there. Maybe those wild passionate nights or sweet, languid mornings?" She was talking out of her ass and knew it.

Christy-Anne was growling. Finally, she sighed. "He did cook me breakfast once."

"See? There's something."

"It was terrible."

"It's the thought that counts."

"Whatever. I still want him out of here and out of my life. I can't keep writing songs about the same fucked-up relationship!"

*Actually, you can and you probably will*, Lucille thought but didn't say. Christy-Anne's sappy songs about her broken heart were the only ones that even made it onto the charts. Her "clubbin' hits" and songs about what it was like to be rich in Vegas remained buried on her albums, only discovered by die-hard fans. "All right, I'll talk to Ryan, invent some reason for him to move out, and then we'll get your life back to normal."

Christy-Anne stopped growling. "Finally. I swear, if you do this for me, I'll never fire you again. You can be my publicist for the rest of both our lives."

"Yeah," Lucille said, gritting her teeth at the thought. An hour and an agonizing conversation with Ryan later, she got him to move out that night. She had to promise him a rumored affair with the model Mariah, though. Now she'd have to call Mariah to work that out. Her job never ended.

Though her main sources of steady income had just decided to part ways, all she felt was relief and a heavy dose of dread. They'd both promised to work with her for the rest of their lives.

Brett couldn't believe where he was going. He opened his mouth to tell the cab driver to turn around and take him back to the mansion, but Simon Anton was staying there, "keeping an eye on things," and Brett got the feeling he was no longer wanted. He'd emerged from his drug haze to find himself in the spare bedroom, still wearing Michel's oversized suit, a bag from his apartment sitting at the foot of the bed. With the help of one of Michel's male staff members, who seemed to all be back to work, he was able to shower and get dressed in his jeans and a faded red t-shirt. His arm throbbed from its two-day ordeal, but at least the dressing was new and the bone had been properly set the second time. That information came from Michel, since Brett didn't remember much after the elevator kissing.

Now the two of them, Simon and Michel, were in the courtyard, supposedly discussing their course of action. What they appeared to be doing was drinking and talking about Michel's body of work. Simon Anton, no surprise, was a huge fan of Michel and even owned his Italian-language love song album—both of them.

They hadn't noticed when Brett had left the house, even though he'd made no attempt to be quiet. It wasn't so much that he wanted them to know he was leaving, but because he didn't want potential murderers mistaking him for Michel again. He had been making a habit of announcing his name and his status as Sylvia's cousin every time he entered a room. He knew Simon's story was a bunch of bull. Though he didn't know his cousin Sylvia well, he doubted she'd stoop to doing anything as virtuous as protecting Michel. Nor would she ever risk her own life to save his. Something foul was at play, so he was going to find the one person who could tell him what.

Well, that wasn't the only reason he was going to find her...

The cab stopped outside a medium-sized, pale-gray house in a suburb on the outside of the city. Brett frowned at the house. The siding was all wood, and the railing up to the porch looked Victorian in design. An old house. In this town. The rest of the suburb was the same, a few new houses mixed in, but for the most part older houses with stone chimneys and wrap-around porches. It was not at all what he'd expected of her.

He paid the driver and walked to the front door. It opened soon after he knocked to reveal a glaring Lucille in another of those short dresses he liked so much—bare feet and no makeup. If his arm weren't in a sling...

"Oh, of course they sent you," she said by way of a greeting.

"Who sent me?" He was genuinely confused.

"My uncle." She looked at him like he was being stupid. "Bastard must have had me followed."

Brett shook his head. "Uh, no. He didn't. I mean, I got your address from him, yes, but he didn't send me."

Lucille sighed and pulled him inside, closing the door behind him. The interior made even less sense. There were beautiful hardwood floors and paintings on the wall. The living room had soft, comfortable couches and a Persian rug. There was a huge bookcase on one side of the room and a crystal chandelier dangling from the high ceiling.

"Um," he began, "your house..."

She looked at him, the glare turning into something lighter. "It's awful, isn't it? It's not mine. I have to move a lot, what with the whole secret job and all. The more a place looks like somewhere I'd never live, the better a cover it is."

"Oh thank God. This place looks like the perfect spot to raise a family," Brett said with a shudder.

She grimaced and put her finger to his lips. "Shut up. Don't ever say that to me again."

He grinned.

Lucille dropped her finger and turned toward the ridiculous antique liquor cabinet in the corner. "Do you want a drink?"

Brett, heady from having her stand so close to him, shook his head. She didn't see it, pondering the decanters in front of her. "No," he said, his voice a little hoarse. *How embarrassing.*

She turned around, her eyebrows raised. "You don't want a drink? I thought you were supposed to be a tormented, alcoholic screenwriter?"

"Yeah, supposed to be," Brett said absently, his mind not on writing.

Lucille didn't say anything, but walked over to sit in one of the high-backed Victorian chairs. She watched him.

Brett realized she was waiting for a better answer than, "Yeah, supposed to be." He shifted, still standing near the door, too uncomfortable to sit down. Then he began with a huge, dramatic sigh.

"The tortured artist thing is really my family's idea. I never wanted to be an alcoholic writer, but it's kind of the family business. My dad's one, my brother, my sisters, my grandfather's one, his father was one. It goes back centuries."

"Jesus."

"I know."

"Your family wanted you to be an alcoholic?"

Brett nodded. "Yep. Though that's the main reason I'm not speaking to any of them right now. They're all in and out of rehab."

"What about your mom?"

"She...um...runs the Michel Polce Stalker Society." Brett winced as he said this. From what little he knew of Lucille's family, it wasn't like they were perfect, but his was really fucked up. Never more so than when he talked about them out loud.

"I'm just going to leave that one alone."

Brett nodded. "For the best."

She put on a wicked smirk, stood up, and sauntered over to him. She trailed her hand lightly up his arm, leaving goosebumps. "You know what we haven't gotten to do..."

Brett went to touch her, to grab her. Then he stopped and dropped his hand. He felt uncertain and nervous, like he was his seventeen-year-old self, about to lose it to Amber Whitfield in her bedroom while their parents were at a PTA meeting. "Are you sure about this?"

"It's just sex," she whispered in his ear. She took his earlobe between her teeth and tugged. Brett groaned.

She kissed down his neck, walking them backward to the living room wall. There she pushed him against it and claimed his mouth, pressing every inch of her body against his as she did so.

Brett pulled back as much as he could, disentangling his mouth from hers. "Wait."

"What? What could you possibly have to tell me right now?"

"Um, with this arm, I won't really, uh, be able to do much passionate throwing-you-down-on-the-bed or whatever."

Lucille laughed, and the sound vibrating through him was arousing. "I don't think that's going to be a problem."

"Why not?" He was once again genuinely confused.

She looked him in the eye with a bemused smile. "Because you're going to be the one getting thrown down on the bed. And I'm always in control," she whispered again, the soft pressure of her lips making him close his eyes and groan.

Brett swallowed. Something about her taking control—really, everything about her taking control—was the sexiest thing he'd ever heard. He'd never been one of those men who had to assert his dominance through being on top or bondage or whatever. Some women had wanted him to, so he had. But it had never felt quite like this.

Her hands were under his t-shirt before he stopped thinking. She pushed it up, over his stomach, until it caught on his sling. She reached up and removed the sling, not gently like in the hotel, but hurried, desperate, impatient.

He winced but helped her get it off. That obstacle out of the way, she pulled his shirt over his head and then set to work on his jeans. He put his hand on her arm; this was going too fast. Sure, he was ready, he'd been ready since they'd started making out against the wall, but he wanted to enjoy this, his first time with this gorgeous, powerful woman.

"Wait, slow down," he said.

She looked up at him, her eyes full of desire. "Dear God, why?"

"I just...want to enjoy it."

She leaned in, running her hands up his chest as she did so, and kissed him. Her tongue licked the outside of his lips and then slid inside, playing with his. He moaned and kissed her back, hard. It wasn't until his pants fell to his ankles that he pulled back, breathing heavily.

"Hey, you don't play fair," he gasped.

"I never said I did." She whispered the words against his lips, and his brain shut up again.

With his free hand, he reached behind her neck and tried to undo the halter top of her dress. He couldn't do it one-handed.

Lucille stepped back and smiled seductively at him. She quickly untied her dress and shimmied out of it. Underneath she wore a strapless bra and black, lacy underwear. He swallowed, standing there in his boxers, his jeans around his ankles.

They stared at each other for a long second, and then Lucille jumped him again, slamming him hard against the wall. He groaned, this time from the pain, but it was lost in her kisses. His blood pounded through his body, his erection pressing eagerly against her. She was shorter than him, though, so it pressed against her belly and not that sweet spot between her thighs.

He pulled back again, this time with reluctance, his good arm pushing gently on her shoulder, his bad one useless. "Luce."

Lucille glared at him this time, her chest heaving, each breath making her strapless bra slide down a few millimeters, revealing more of her breasts.

He almost pulled her back in right then and there—picked her up, wrapped her legs around his waist, and let her ride him against the wall. He would have, too, if the logistics wouldn't have gotten in the way.

"Do not tell me to slow down again," Lucille hissed.

"Uh, no. I got the impression that was off the table."

"Then what?"

"Which way to the bedroom? Because as much as I'd love to pick you up and, uh..." It was the most awkward conversation he'd ever had. Who stopped in the middle of sex to talk about logistics? And what word should he use? "Fucking" sounded too crude. They weren't making love. Screwing? Banging? Making the beast with two backs? All great for telling your best guy friends about your romantic indiscretions later, but in the heat of the moment they sounded crass. "Uh, have sex against this wall, but it's a little impossible right now." He gestured at his arm.

Lucille's glare disappeared. She smiled at him—not the cocky grin from earlier, but something a little softer. She grabbed his hand. "Well, come on then."

He didn't move, not yet. She looked back at him, impatient.

"I just don't want to trip over my pants," he said lamely.

She laughed. "You're adorable." Then she helped him out of his jeans and led him up to her bedroom.

*Adorable?* He'd never been called adorable in his life and didn't know what to make of it. He told his brain to shut up and get busy with the mostly naked woman in front of him instead.

In the upstairs hall, Lucille turned around and kissed him again. She maneuvered them so she was pushing him backwards, their legs tangling together, their mouths attached. They almost didn't make it to the bed and probably wouldn't have if Brett's arm hadn't been an issue. She slammed him against her bedroom door, opening it with the force of the impact. He groaned against her mouth again, this time in pain and pleasure. No doubt he'd have a bruise tomorrow, but he'd stopped caring.

His knees hit the back of the bed and folded, bringing him down on his back. He used his good arm to pull Lucille down on top of him.

She disentangled herself and sat up, straddling his hips. Reaching around, she undid the clasp of her bra, letting it fall off to reveal two of the most perfect breasts he'd ever seen. Well, almost perfect. The left one had a condom stuck to it.

He laughed, unable to help himself. She smacked him on the shoulder.

"Hey," he said.

"Well."

"You have a condom stuck to your boob."

Lucille looked down and peeled the condom off her breast. She wasn't surprised to see it there. "I know. That's where I keep them."

"Who keeps a condom in their bra?" Brett asked, still grinning.

She grinned back and held up the Girl Scout salute. "Always be prepared. You never know what could happen where. Girl Scout's honor."

"No way were you a Girl Scout."

She winked at him.

His brain processed the rest of her words. Thinking about Lucille being prepared to have sex any-where with anyone didn't help his feelings of inadequacy. There was no way to misinterpret her words. He remembered her being adamantly opposed to plane sex, the type of adamant that came from prior experience. He knew this wasn't special and didn't mean anything, but he couldn't help feeling let down.

Then Lucille moved her hips, grinding them against his erection. He decided to ignore those feelings for now in favor of the other, much better feelings that were going on wherever she touched him.

How she'd gotten their underwear off, he didn't know. It was sometime during the making out. Next thing he did know, she'd gotten the condom on and was riding him, hard and fast. He decided he liked this position—he could watch her and have easy access to her breasts and her clit. However, at the pace she'd set, he barely got his finger down to stroke her when he came, unexpected and uncontrollably. He couldn't hold on. The sight of her above him, her head thrown back, her body all around him, had sent him over the edge without a parachute.

Lucille collapsed against him, breathing hard, her sweat mingling with his, her legs still clenched around him. She lifted her head and kissed him before rolling off him and standing up. She walked to the ensuite bathroom, completely naked, and closed the door behind her.

Brett lay on her bed, stunned. He felt sated but not satisfied. Had she even come? He hated to admit he didn't know.

That was not how he'd imagined his first time with Lucille would go. And he'd been thinking about that first time nonstop since he'd crashed into Michel's hotel room three nights ago. Kissing? Yes. Gratuitous touching? Definitely. But in his mind it was more fun. Not a wham, bam, thank you ma'am sort of a deal. Not an embarrassing loss of control like a teenage virgin.

He sighed and scowled at the crown molding. Then he stripped off the used condom and deposited it into the bedside trash just as the bathroom door opened.

Lucille walked back out from bathroom and started putting her lingerie back on.

Brett no longer felt like a boy who'd just lost his virginity. He felt like the high school girl who'd slept with the coolest boy in school only to discover he'd been using her for sex and wasn't actually going to ask her to the prom. Which was stupid, since he'd known this was just sex from the beginning.

He sat up and picked his boxers off the floor. "Next time, I think we should go slow," he said, more to himself than her. He didn't realize he'd spoken so loud until he caught sight of her face.

Judging by the stony, unreadable look she was giving him, it was the wrong thing to say.

# CHAPTER SEVENTEEN

I t hadn't been mind-blowing sex. Yes, Brett had come fast, and she'd had to hurry to keep up. They'd both orgasmed, which was supposed to be the sign of success. *If it is why does Brett look like he's been used, and why do I feel like I took advantage of him?* When she'd escaped to the bathroom, it was to look at herself in the mirror and give herself a stern talking to about projecting emotions that weren't there. There were facts she couldn't ignore, such as how gentle his hand was when he ran it over her skin, how much it felt like a caress instead of a feel-up. Or how soft and delicious his lips were, like eating a fresh strawberry. Lucille hadn't savored. She couldn't. She hadn't wanted his soft caress or his tasty mouth. She had wanted a quick, hard fuck to get over this sexual tension between them, and that was what they'd done. Now Brett was screwing that up with his next-time talk.

He'd frozen after saying those words, one leg through his boxers, still naked. She didn't want to have this conversation with him while he was naked, dammit. He looked good naked. Really good.

Lucille chose her words carefully. She didn't want to hurt him—he didn't deserve that. "You do understand the concept of a one-time thing, right?"

Brett finished putting on his boxers. "Of course I do," he grumbled.

"Good." She thought about asking if they were good, but she didn't need to. Michel was no longer her client, so there was no reason for her to see Brett again. Her stomach churned.

"I just figured... Never mind." Brett didn't look at her.

"What?"

"I said, never mind."

Lucille growled and put her hands on her bare hips. "Brett Jacobs. I may have only known you for a few days, but I've never known you to hold back your opinion. So let's hear it."

Brett stood up. He was watching her now, and she couldn't stand it. His gaze made the hair on her arms stand up and a flush travel over her body, warming her from the inside out. She stared at the wall with its stupid, gilded landscape painting.

Brett sighed. "I don't think that was satisfying for either of us."

She turned to glare at him at that. "What the fuck? Was it my imagination that you came? Because I certainly did."

"Great, yeah, no, it was great. But I think we, this, could be amazing, you know? If we gave it a chance, a real chance," Brett's words came out in a rush. He rambled, saying things that Lucille didn't want to hear. As he spoke, he walked closer to her, reaching out his good arm. When he was right in front of her, he tucked her hair behind her ear with that arm, allowing his hand to linger on her cheek.

Lucille scoffed. "That sounds like a bad R&B song."

"You make me feel like a bad R&B song."

She didn't know what to say to that. There wasn't room to say anything because he leaned down and kissed her softly on the lips. Softly with those succulent strawberry lips. When she was a kid, she used to love finding wild strawberries in the woods behind her grandparents' house, the mansion in the country that had been passed down to her mother on their death and that had sat empty ever since. The strawberries had arrived with her in the early summer, hidden between the overgrown bushes at the edge of the manicured lawn. When the adults were distracted with cocktails and cards, she'd sneak out to those woods, alone and fearless. When she'd found her prize, she'd always follow the same little ritual. She'd pick the berry off the vine, blow on it, whisper a wish, close her eyes tightly, bite into it, and fall to the ground in a dramatic swoon, the juice running down her lips and onto the ground around her. This routine could be repeated twenty or more times in an evening, depending on the availability of the berries and the time before her grandma called her to dinner. After each swoon, she'd wait on the ground until her fantasy prince came and kissed her back to life. And since he was fantasy, he always came.

Lucille had bitten the strawberry and felt her body go lax, leaning into the arms of the fantasy prince. He tasted so real, so alive this time, in a way he never had when she was a girl. She nibbled the strawberry, her teeth nipping at it. Brett's moan in response brought her back to reality, back to his arms, back to kissing him. She pushed him away.

"No," she said.

Brett looked startled, but he recovered and tried to cross his arms over his bare chest, forgetting about the injured one. "Why not?"

"A, I don't date celebrities, even D-listers like yourself. B, I don't date, period. C, I think you'd be better off finding some nice girl who'll be your muse and help you kick your drinking problem and who wants to get married and have babies and all that shit." Lucille was still breathing heavily. She was aroused and annoyed, and, judging by the less than concealing coverage of his boxers, Brett was the same.

"What if I don't want any of that stuff?" Brett looked really pissed now.

"You do, I know you do. Look at how you showed up to help Michel even though he hadn't talked to you in years." Lucille was scrambling for reasons and hated how flustered she felt.

"I showed up to kick his ass. The only reason I helped him at all was because I honestly had nothing better to do." Brett scowled. "At least at first. Now I'm around because I want to see you. Only you quit, so I don't really know what the point is anymore."

It was the least romantic thing anyone had ever said to her, and her heart warmed. "I'm not a nice girl."

Brett's scowl deepened. "I know. I don't care."

Lucille sighed. She wanted to wring his neck and fuck him. *Like choke sex,* her mind offered.

"Here's the way I see it. You've been lonely and bored for a long time now. You wanted an adventure, but it didn't turn out to be the adventure you thought it would be, so you're mad. You wanted a boy toy, but I didn't turn out to be what you thought either, and that scares you. You're scared and mad and lonely and sick of being everyone's fucking life vest."

If she could bristle any more, she did. "None of that's true."

"Isn't it?"

"I love my job."

"You've been ignoring your phone ever since you got on that plane."

"So?"

Brett was angry.

Was she? It was hard to keep track.

"I think you want something more. I think you want something real. I'm real and I'm here and I've never pretended to be anything I'm not."

She scoffed. "Well, that's true."

Brett's eyes narrowed. "When life finally bites you in the ass, sweetie, I am not going to be the one applying the ointment."

"Fine."

"Fine."

They stood there, both breathing heavily, both still aroused, Brett obviously so. Lucille didn't know who moved first, but the next moment, they were in each other's arms, kissing as though their lives depended on it. Brett grabbed her with his good hand and ground his hips into hers, making her gasp into his persistent mouth. When he brought his tongue into play, she went weak in the knees, grabbing his hair and digging her nails into his back to help her stay upright. Brett moaned again, but this time she didn't stop. She couldn't stop, not when they were so far gone.

Brett turned them and pushed her onto the bed, landing on top of her, gracelessly and heavy.

"Oof."

"Sorry," he whispered, also grimacing. He must have landed on his injured arm. "I keep forgetting about this thing."

"Probably just needs a little attention," Lucille whispered back, feeling wicked. She pushed down his boxers with her feet and reached between them to grasp him, running her hand up and down his length.

"That's not what I meant and you know it," Brett growled, working hard to speak between groans of pleasure.

She took her hand away.

"Don't stop," he begged, looking down at her with wide eyes.

She giggled, actually giggled, as she pulled him down to kiss, her hand continuing its exploration.

Brett pulled back a few moments later. "Too many clothes."

"What?"

"You're wearing too many clothes," he said, rolling them over so she was straddling him. He undid her bra, pulling it off slowly, meeting her eyes the whole time.

Lucille shivered from the intimacy. She almost stopped it right then and there. Then he put his mouth on one of her nipples, and all the reasons to stop escaped her as she arched into his caress.

Her underwear soon met the same fate as the bra, thrown to the side in the haste of needing to feel skin against skin.

"You don't by chance have another condom hidden in these?" he asked, fondling her breasts to make sure.

She laughed. "I have one in the bed stand."

He reached awkwardly for the drawer with his working arm, his chest rubbing against her. If she bent over, she could lick him. She did. He tasted sweaty in a sexy, manly way. She ground her hips against his to speed up his search.

He returned, foil-wrapped packet in his good hand. "That's not playing fair."

Lucille was about to apologize but got distracted by him putting on the condom, kissing her, lifting her hips, and then entering her all in quick succession. They took it slow, moving together to hit those spots that had them both gasping. When he angled her above him so he could reach between them to touch her, she came with a small cry, his name on her lips. He followed soon after, pulling her against him and calling out her name.

Afterward, they lay in the bed, gasping, limbs and sheets tangled, a comatose pair of sexually satisfied bodies. Lucille lay her head on Brett's chest, feeling him try to catch his breath, his heart pounding away beside her ear. For a few blissful seconds, her brain stayed in its post-orgasmic daze.

Then it started thinking again. She sat up and looked down into Brett's face, frowning.

Brett frowned back at her. "It's time to start arguing again, isn't it?"

"This"—she indicated their naked, sweaty, intertwined bodies—"was not part of the plan." She pushed herself off the bed and put her bra back on.

Who knew what had happened to her underwear. That and her dress was still downstairs. She grabbed a pair of clean undies and jeans from her dresser and shimmied into them, all the while aware of Brett watching her but refusing to meet his gaze.

Brett sat up. "But it could be, you know?" He got up, trashing the condom, and replaced his boxers. "We don't have to be serious. We could be, you know, fuck buddies."

Lucille cringed at the idea but didn't know why. All she had were fuck buddies. "I don't think that would work."

"Why not?"

"I don't know! Just someday you'll want more and I won't be able to give you more and then you'll be heartbroken and I'll feel bad for breaking your heart."

"Christ, that sounds terrible."

"I know. Which is why we shouldn't do it."

Brett looked thoughtful. "Or, alternative scenario, what if we were fuck buddies and I didn't want more ever and we went on like this?"

"Uh huh, right. And how many successful FB relationships have you seen?"

"Well...okay, but why is it me who starts to feel more? Why wouldn't it be you? How I see it is you have just as much chance of falling in love with me as I do with you."

Lucille didn't get to tell him how ridiculous that was because she'd had many successful hookups. The front door opened and closed. They froze, their eyes wide, staring at each other.

Before they could heroically try to save each other, Simon's voice called, "Lucy, why the hell is your front door unlocked? Anyone could have walked in. Like I just did."

# Chapter Eighteen

A moment later: "And who the hell's pants are these? Do you have company?"

There was the sound of footsteps on the stairs, and Simon walked into her bedroom before they could even start breathing again. He stopped in the doorway and took in the scene before him. Lucille pictured it through his eyes as he stood there in his skinny jeans and black leather jacket, still wearing his aviator sunglasses. Her ugly room with its gilded landscape paintings and hardwood furniture, the four-poster bed taking up most of the floor space. And in the middle of it, her, wearing jeans but no shirt, with sex hair and no makeup; Brett standing in front of her in only his boxers, his hair no neater than hers; both of them startled and looking more than a little bit guilty.

Simon pulled off his glasses slowly and raised an eyebrow at them. "Huh," he said after a long silence.

"What?" Lucille hid her embarrassment behind a scowl. It wasn't hard, considering how much she'd been scowling at Brett. It was starting to feel natural to her muscles now. "Whatever you're thinking, just say it and get it over with."

"I did not see that coming."

Brett was also scowling, his arms awkwardly folded across his chest. "What didn't you see coming? That your darling niece would have an affair with someone like me?"

"God, no. Lucy's banged way worse."

She snorted. "You're one to talk."

"Face it, my dear, we're a family of sluts."

"Truer words were never spoken." She stopped scowling. She wasn't mad at Simon, not really. A little bit for abandoning her for eight years and for the stuff earlier on the plane, but not about this. She needed to keep her annoyance focused on where it belonged: the mostly naked guy standing next to her who she still wanted to fuck and punch at the same time. That would make an interesting sport. Or reality TV show—*Fuck Punch.*

Brett was still caught up on the semantics. "Then what do you mean by what you said?"

Simon shrugged. "I'd thought you were gay and that you had a huge gay crush on Michel."

Brett's face turned red. "I'm not gay."

Lucille could have told him that. Simon, not Brett. Brett already knew he wasn't gay. She tried not to smile, knowing it would make Brett madder. But then she remembered she wanted to make him mad. She smiled.

"Bi?"

"No."

Simon shrugged. "Oh well. I just assumed, given the strop you were in about him never being around and what not, and how willing you were to put yourself in harm's way for him, that there was at least a little something going on."

"I am not willing to put myself in harm's way for him."

"Then how do you explain the arm? And the bomb?"

Brett's face was bright red, borderline purple. "I didn't want to get my shoulder dislocated! I wasn't the one who screwed up and got the wrong guy! And you're the one who set off the bomb!"

"Details," Simon said with a wave of his hand.

"Look. Lucille and I were in the middle of something. Leave," Brett said through his teeth.

Lucille spoke up then. This was an out, and she wasn't going to let it go by. "We were finished. Stay."

Brett looked at her. All the indignation and anger had drained from his face, leaving behind a dull, unreadable look. "I thought we were still discussing—"

"We weren't. What's done is done. I think it's time for you to go." Lucille kept her face stoic and emotionless. It wasn't hard; she'd had years of practice. She felt weird, sort of blank inside, empty. She felt distanced from the situation and the man before her, like it was happening to someone else.

"Okay," was all Brett said. He walked past Simon, careful not to touch him, his shoulders slumped. She heard him walk down the stairs, the sound of his clothes rustling as he struggled to dress himself, and the front door close behind him.

Lucille didn't say anything, though her mind was tumbling with questions for her uncle. Her heart hurt. And she'd identified the weird feeling—it was like kicking a kitten. Which was stupid and crazy because Brett wasn't a kitten. He was a drunken, slovenly failure who was so far outside of her normal type, she hadn't known men like him existed before now. But he was funny and caring and incredibly loyal. And he was sarcastic and ironic, couldn't think on his feet for shit, and he wanted her, all of her. He wanted to make love to her, slowly, languidly, like they had a lifetime to get it right. Goddamn him and his cute butt.

"That was really weird, Lucy."

Lucille turned her attention to Simon. "Aren't you supposed to be watching Michel?"

"He's a big boy. He can take care of himself."

Lucille shook her head. "He really can't. Why do you think Brett was living there? And we took him with us to the island? It wasn't for his spy skills."

"I assumed it was for his hot bod, but after what I walked in on just now..." Simon trailed off, indicating he wasn't sure what to make of Lucille's choice in men.

Whatever. She didn't need his approval. Not that she was choosing Brett, but if she were, she wouldn't care what Simon thought. "I'm going to put on a shirt and then you're going to tell me what you're doing here."

"Can't an uncle come visit his favorite niece?"

She gave him a look.

"I swear, my call is entirely social. I'll be downstairs." Simon exited, leaving the door open.

She could hear him rooting around her living room, then the clink of glass and ice. She sighed and grabbed the first shirt from her closet. It was a red button-down blouse with fitted panels that accented her waist and chest. She swapped her jeans out for her black pants and surveyed herself in the mirror. She felt professional, confident, and collected, almost enough to deal with her uncle. The flippant, flirty Lucille in her short silky dress, ready to bang the first guy who walked through the door, was gone. Now she was back and all business.

A thought hit her, like pain medication finally kicking in. It was one of those epiphany moments when everything clicked into place and the last, lost piece to the puzzle, the one that was hiding behind the toilet for six months, finally found its home. Before she lost her nerve or the feeling of giddy weightless freedom that had accompanied her re-alization, she went to confront her uncle.

When she walked downstairs, Simon was perched in one of the overstuffed chairs in the living room. "The one brilliant thing about the Victorians, and I do mean the *one* thing, was their ability to craft a liquor cabinet."

Lucille didn't respond. She sat down on the chair facing him, mirroring his relaxed but ready stance. "Simon," she started out, "you know I'd do anything for you, right?"

He nodded but narrowed his eyes. "Why are you dressed like that? What do you want from me?"

She rolled her eyes. "You're always so suspicious of my motives."

"Aren't you of mine? It's the business, darling."

"That's what I want to talk about. You want to come back and pick up your old life, right? Be a celebrity spin doctor again?" Lucille was trying to tread carefully. Her future could rest on the way she chose her words.

"More than anything." His words were whispered, hopeful.

"Good. So what do we need to do to get your name cleared?" she asked in a rush.

Simon blinked. She'd stumped him. Under other circumstances, she'd have gloated. Now she needed him to keep up.

"What do you mean?"

The rest came pouring out. "I mean, I don't want to do this anymore. I don't want to be Lucille Anton, Celebrity Spin Doctor. When I was on the island, I had a team, and we were working together, sort of, and we were doing something, kind of. I got to wear whatever I wanted—"

"Yeah, about that dress—"

"—and be around people who knew me. People who I wasn't trying to play or manipulate or con. You know?"

Silence.

"Not really. But let's pretend I do."

"Close enough." And it was. For her uncle, a man who lived for parties, manipulation, and scandal, even pretending he knew what she was talking about would do. She couldn't tell him about her loneliness or how she wanted real friends—those were things he wouldn't understand. She didn't tell him that she'd spent the last eight years running on guilt and an inflated sense of responsibility. And she especially wouldn't tell him that she was starting to think of Michel and Brett as her weird, dysfunctional family. She wasn't even ready to admit that to herself. "So what do we do to clear your name? Assuming that you are, in fact, innocent."

Simon watched her for a full minute before answering. "You know, Lucy, most of the time I'm lying through my teeth. But this was the one thing I was truthful about, and it kills me that it's what I got exiled for."

"You didn't get exiled. You fled."

Simon waved his hand. "Semantics. As for how we clear my name, that's simple." He took a long, slow drink of his scotch before he continued. "We need to kill Beverly."

Lucille, who'd leaned forward as she explained her new life realization, sat back hard in the chair.

"We need to what?" She tried to process. "Who the fuck is Beverly? Why do we need to kill her? Because won't that defeat the whole purpose of clearing your name?"

"Not kill her, *kill* her. We need to kill her reputation, get the truth out of her, get her to fess up to the crime. Perhaps 'kill' was not the right word."

"'Kill' was definitely not the right word."

Simon didn't respond. He contemplated his glass with the intensity of a man thinking of other things.

Lucille waited. Her fingernails needed to be dealt with. That manicure had been years ago, judging by the state of them. Of course, if this all worked out and she passed the business back to Simon, would she need manicures anymore? Would she need any of it anymore? Her car, her wardrobe, the houses she had on retainer? The panic bubbled up in her throat. She was making a huge mistake in giving up her livelihood. After all, she hadn't done well in college, didn't have any experience in anything legitimate, had never even worked a summer job babysitting! She was unqualified, undereducated, and any other 'un' words she could think of at everything except spin doctoring.

Simon broke through her internal freak-out. "I suppose you want to know what really happened eight years ago."

"Yeah, sure," she said around the lump of terror. If she wanted to take back her words, the time was now. She'd open her mouth and say, *Thanks, but never mind, I want the business.* Lucille thought of the honest, hopeful look on her uncle's face when she'd offered him his life back. *Goddammit.*

Simon closed his eyes, toying with the glass as he spoke. "It started about ten years ago. I'd taken on one of those cases; you know the kind, the ones you know you should stay away from but can't?"

She nodded, her mind still churning.

"His name was Cooper—"

"The murdered guy."

"Right. Yes, well, he was still alive then. Cooper was into some weird sexual shit—BDSM, orgies, making pornos, everything except bestiality; that was where he drew the line."

Lucille grimaced. "No wonder you didn't tell me about it." When she'd first started out, she would have thought this Cooper as a real whack job. Now she simply appreciated not having to work with him.

"Right? Well, you had started dating that cop, and a lot of this stuff wasn't just kinky, it was illegal. Drugs, prostitutes... Anyway, you know the story—big star who didn't want people to know what was happening behind closed doors, et cetera." Simon poured another drink. "One of the parties, an orgy, went horribly wrong. I won't traumatize you with the details. If I could forget them myself, I absolutely would. It would cut down on at least three of my sleeping pills." He took a long drink of his scotch.

Lucille's heart rate had returned to normal as she listened. The panic was passing. She found her uncle's story comforting in a twisted sort of way. It was comforting to think that, no matter what she'd be doing from here on out, it wouldn't involve unstable celebrities and their deviant behavior. "Did someone die?"

Simon nodded. "Yeah, and it was gruesome. When I saw Cooper soon after, he was still shaken from it. He came to see me one night at the house."

Lucille remembered that night. It had been the night her life had gone belly up. It had been summertime, she was learning the family business by day and sneaking out to see Matt at night. Simon had hated Matt, even before he had real reason to. The sneaking around allowed Simon to conveniently ignore Matt as much as he wanted, until that night.

It had been late—Lucille had just said good night to Matt and climbed in through the window.

She'd heard voices downstairs and had crept to the railing. Simon had been standing in the hallway, wearing a red smoking jacket and black lounge pants, the closest he got to casual. She'd been able to see his face, and he'd looked concerned, his hand on the arm of the man whose back had been to her. A taller, dark-haired man with slumped shoulders. Her uncle had seen her right away, before she'd been able to make out what the stranger had been saying. His eyes had ordered her to go back in her room, and she'd done so. Her uncle had never been strict—so when he'd wanted her to do something, it was for her own protection. The first rule he'd taught her was to keep the ones you love at a distance. To let them in was to put them at risk. What she had picked up was that the man had been in a panic, talking fast and crying.

"There was a video. Cooper liked to film his parties. He had it and he wanted to go to the police with it. He was terrified that it hadn't been an accident and he was going to be next. There were five people, including the victim and himself, who could be identified on that video."

"One of them was Beverly?"

"One of them was Beverly. Beverly Walton, your typical up-and-coming model with everything to lose. She was in a dozen ad campaigns that summer alone, and she was a frequent attendee at Cooper's parties."

"She was the one who killed the person in the orgy."

Simon paused. "No. I mean, I don't know. I never saw the video, and Cooper never said."

"Then why do we need to find her?"

"Because," he said, gripping his glass, "she murdered Cooper."

Not even two minutes after Lucille had closed her bedroom door, there'd been a gunshot and yelling. She hadn't been able to ignore it, her heart pounding as she'd imagined that tall man killing her uncle again and again. Only when she'd reached the stair landing, the tall man had been the one who'd lain dead, and it had been her uncle being cuffed and led away. Cuffed by none other than her off-duty cop boyfriend who'd come back for one final good-night kiss.

Throughout the trial, Lucille had stood by her uncle. She'd known nothing about Cooper or how Simon had been involved, so it hadn't been hard to tell the truth. She hadn't lied when she'd said her uncle wasn't capable of killing an unarmed man in cold blood. Even when Matt, wearing a wire and using their relationship as a weapon, had tried to get her to break, she hadn't. But she'd always wondered. The evidence, and lack of evidence, had been overwhelming against her uncle. Simon had been given life in prison and would have been there now if he hadn't escaped, using connections she knew nothing about.

"You thought I did it," Simon said. He was watching her again, as though trying to see inside her mind while she processed the bombshells.

"I didn't know," she answered honestly.

He smiled. "Smart girl. But you never talked. I couldn't have been more proud of you."

She smiled back. "Thanks. You know, other families are proud of good grades and trophies. We're proud of being able to keep our mouths shut."

Simon laughed. "I know. We'd be great in the mob."

Lucille laughed too. It felt weird and right, and she doubted anyone but the two of them would understand. "So, what really happened that night?"

"While I was trying to talk Cooper out of going to the police until we could figure out a strategy that would involve keeping him safe and everyone's reputation intact, Beverly opened the front door, shot him, and bolted."

"Don't they have ballistics tests for things like that? And fingerprinting?"

Simon sighed. "The bitch shot him from right beside me. Cooper didn't see her since he was a blubbering, snotty mess, rest his soul. She used a gun from my father's collection. She wore gloves so there were no discernible fingerprints.

"Anyway, first there was all this racket and Cooper's bleeding out and my eardrums are completely shot. Then your boyfriend shows up with his handcuffs and police buddies to find me standing over the dying man, a smoking gun on the floor, and no sign of Beverly. Well, you remember the rest."

Lucille nodded. "Vividly. I was so pissed at Matt for arresting you I broke up with him over it."

Simon threw back his head and laughed. "I'd have liked to see that."

She smirked. "It was good. Horrible at the time. I thought I was in love with him. But he honestly had no idea what he did wrong. Like arresting my only family was no big deal."

"Men."

She nodded. "Okay, so what do we need to do?"

Simon smiled. "Do you still have your black uni-tard?"

# Chapter Nineteen

Brett went back to his apartment. In times of great upheaval and stress, a man needed his home. His home was his castle. But when he heaved himself through the scratched white door that always stuck, the sight within was less than comforting.

"This place is a dump," he said to the piles of dirty clothes and dishes in his path. He stood in the doorway, surveying his garbage can of a castle. Something inside of him snapped. He could either leave, walk away from his mess, and pretend it didn't exist, or he could stay and deal with it. There was nowhere to walk to. He couldn't handle Michel's drama, and he'd burned his bridge to Lucille. The sad truth of it was, he had no one else to turn to. No other friends. His family—was he not speaking to them, or had they cut him off? Both were likely, and either way, they were unavailable.

He hadn't noticed before that he lived in such squalor. Michel had told him as much a few nights back when he'd arrived to pick up Brett for their sleepover. This new awareness could be because, apart from the pain meds he'd left at Michel's, he hadn't had anything in the past twenty-four hours. Not a drop of liquor. He was perfectly, horribly sober, staring at the manifestation of his shitty life.

He began to clean. This wasn't an eighties movie montage with friends and a great soundtrack. It was grueling, silent, and long. His iPod was broken and he was alone.

Once the clothes and dishes were cleared and the empty whiskey bottles and beer cans recycled, he found his layer of discarded drafts. The sequel to *The Night Before the Apocalypse*, now so long overdue he'd been dropped by the studio and his agent, abandoned by the few fans he had, and rejected by the girl he loved. The last didn't have anything to do with his film, but it seemed fitting to include in his laundry list of life failures.

He stuffed the crumpled pieces of paper in a bag and tied it closed. This wasn't one of those moments when he would unfold his work and begin to read with a heavy heart, only to find that the words on the page weren't half as bad as he'd dreaded. That the script only needed tweaking to become the next great thing. No, this was one of those moments when he decided enough was enough. That script would never get written. He hadn't written for days, and he didn't miss it now. That had to be some sort of a sign.

By his bed he found a couple of condom wrappers. He couldn't remember when they were from or who he'd been with. Great. He added banging random girls and not remembering it to his failure list.

On the bed were all of his books. At some point in his drunken slump he'd started sleeping with them, wrapping them around him like an uncomfortably hard and pointy-edged cocoon. Every zombie novel ever written. His collector's edition of *Frankenstein*. Some contemporary mysteries, some classics, some non-fictions about travel and living in the wild. Plus his well-worn chemistry texts, beloved yet abandoned.

Brett put the books back on the empty shelves, turning over each one as he did. They were his grown-up teddy bears. They had been his only comfort when his life bottomed had out. It was time to be an adult again and put them away.

The sheets crinkled when he pulled them back. He almost vomited.

As he put the final touches on his cleaned abode, his cell phone rang. It was charging by the couch in the living room, and he lunged for it, hoping against hope someone had changed her mind and wanted him back. It was Michel.

"Where are you?"

Brett sank down on his couch with his disappointment. "I'm at my place."

"Oh. Why?"

Brett shrugged. Stupid. He was talking on the phone. "I needed to take a step back, and it seemed like you and Simon had everything under control."

"Hmm. We did until Simon disappeared."

"Oh. He's at Lucille's."

There was silence on the other end. Brett realized what he'd said and what he'd admitted to by saying it. He should make up an elaborate excuse.

"You fucked her, didn't you?"

"Yes."

"And Simon walked in on you?"

"Well, yes and no."

"Meaning?"

"Yes, he walked in, but we were mostly clothed already and Lucille was in the middle of stomping on my heart."

There was the sound of running water on Michel's end. "Sorry, bro, that sucks."

"Yeah, wait, what are you doing?" Brett didn't want to know. The words came out of him without his consent.

"I'm taking a bath." This was accompanied by the sound of water swishing, no doubt as Michel climbed into one of his huge Jacuzzi tubs. Naked. While talking on the phone. To Brett.

"Dear God, why?" Brett held the phone away from his ear as though that would protect him from the image of Michel naked in the tub. *No wonder Simon thinks Michel and I have a gay thing going on.* He cringed.

"What else was I supposed to do? You guys all left. Simon's not answering his phone. Lucille won't answer hers. No one's helping me find Sylvia—"

"What do you mean Simon and Lucille aren't answering their phones?" Brett's heart pounded. Even though Lucille had quit, Simon hadn't. With a client like Michel, a fortune-making client, one or both of them should be always available. They were attached at the hip to those phones. It was a compulsion for them. If neither one was answering Michel's calls... He didn't know what it meant yet, but it wasn't something good.

"I mean," Michel was saying, "when I called them, it went to voicemail. So much for 24/7 spin doctor service. I'm in the middle of a major crisis here, and both of the people I'm paying to help me through it have disappeared. Well, I guess one of them was having sex with you, but what about the other?"

"What are you saying?"

"Does Simon Anton strike you as a little off?" Michel asked, splashing again.

"You mean the whole running from the law for eight years without contacting Lucille at all and then trying to blow me up and then helping us, no questions asked?"

"No, I mean, I think he's gay. Of course I mean that!"

Michel was never as dumb as Brett gave him credit for being. Brett's thoughts were reeling. He was trying to piece together everything that had happened in the last few days from the moment he'd stumbled in on Michel and Lucille in the hotel room. He got briefly distracted by thinking about the dress Lucille had been wearing that night but was soon back on track. Still, it wasn't fitting together. It was like a small child's puzzle with those huge wooden pieces that all should fit on the board but don't. He was banging them against the board, over and over again, but with no luck. There was no doubt about it—he wasn't destined for a career as a detective.

"Okay, yeah, that's all kinda iffy. So what do you think is going on?"

His shoulder started to ache in its sling. *Way to choose the worst moment*, he told it sternly.

"I think," Michel said from his Jacuzzi bath, "Simon is the one who kidnapped Sylvia."

Brett, who'd been looking around for something to ease the pain, jumped up. "What? Really? Oh shit, I have to get to Lucille!"

"Um, why?"

"Because, you ass, Simon was with her when I stormed away! If he thinks she knows he's the kidnapper, he may try to take her out!" Brett was pacing the room, yelling into the phone.

"Or they're working together."

Brett paused. It was true. They could be working together. "I'll take my chances. I'd rather be on Lucille's side than against her any day."

"You want a reason to see her again."

"That's crazy."

"Yeah, it is. But whatever. When you're done being crazy, will you please come over? I want to take a nap, but I'm afraid to close my eyes in case someone drops a toaster in my bath or stabs me or something."

With anyone else, Brett could have reassured them they were exaggerating and no one was going to kill them while they slept. With Michel, it was a legitimate concern. "Yeah, sure."

"Hurry." Michel hung up.

Brett grabbed his jacket from its reclaimed hook on the wall. He opened the door to find Sylvia standing on the other side, flanked by two large, sinister-looking men.

"Great timing," she said. "And you're all ready to go. Saves us a lot of work, you know."

Brett was too shocked to do more than mouth words. "But, what, how, why...?"

"You have two options: you can either come with us quietly, or I can have these boys rough you up a little. What do you say, cuz?" She smiled as she spoke. For someone who'd spent the past few days hours kidnapped, Sylvia Stanton looked remarkably well. She was dressed head to toe in black, with smoky eyes and bright red lipstick. There were no rips in her clothes, no tangles in her hair, nothing to indicate she'd been held against her will.

Brett found a bit of his voice to say, "But why me?"

Sylvia smiled wider. "Isn't it obvious? You're the only person I know who's an ordained minister."

# CHAPTER TWENTY

Around the time Brett was startled by Sylvia and her thugs, Lucille waltzed into a hospital, dressed in a commandeered white coat and unfashionable blue scrubs. The unitard had been a joke, but this get-up was hardly better. Simon had a plan. A terrible, simple plan that grew worse and worse the closer she got to the front desk. But it was the only one they had, and this was their one shot, so it had to work.

The security guard behind the desk barely looked up from his computer as Lucille passed, though her footsteps echoed in the empty hallway. *It's working. He thinks I'm a doctor.* The thought had her feeling almost giddy.

She sobered up as she reached the elevators, faced with an array of lettered wings and numbered floors. If she were a real doctor, she would know whether she wanted A7 or B13. Unlike the staff entrance, where she'd scanned her stolen ID card and strolled through undetected, this area wasn't empty. There were people constantly moving. Even in the late hours of the night, the hospital never slept.

Lucille stared down at the clipboard she was carrying, pretending to consult it as she waited for the elevator. "Which floor?" she hissed into the tiny microphone in her cleavage.

Simon's voice crackled in her ear. "I'm working on that."

Lucille sighed and closed her eyes. She had a dozen retorts at the ready, but she was exposed in her current location, and arguing with Simon would only slow him down. Instead, she stared more intently at the blank chart in her hands.

A couple of nurses passed her, chatting together. One of them looked at her with a frown but turned back to the group and continued talking. The elevator arrived. Lucille got in.

"The D wing. She's on the third floor," said Simon in her ear.

Lucille nodded to no one in her empty elevator. When the doors opened again, she stepped out and headed to D, a wing in the back corner of the giant complex, its doors barred from general admittance. The swiped badge got her through and she was inside, standing in the eerie dim light of the psychiatric ward.

Brett was shoved into the back seat of a car. There was a sack over his head and his hands were tied behind his back. Like on a crime show where they find the kidnapped person bound and gagged. Only on those shows, they usually don't reveal said person until they're being saved, and by then the kidnapped person is so grateful, they forget what the hours of bag prison were like. Hot and stuffy was what they were. And smelly. And itchy. The sack they'd put over his head was some sort of old feed bag, the kind used for horses in the movies. It smelled like something earthy and grainy. It itched against his skin, but with his hands bound behind him, he couldn't do a thing about it.

Unfortunately for them, they hadn't gagged him. "Sylvia, where the fuck are you taking me?"

Silence.

"Hello? Sylvia. This is your cousin Brett. The one you just kidnapped? I repeat, where the fuck are you taking me?"

Silence. Then a deep voice, one of the men who'd "helped" him to the car. "Miss Stanton isn't in this vehicle."

"Great. Just great. So where are you bozos taking me then?"

"You'll find out soon enough," the voice replied.

Brett tried to slouch back against the seat, but his hands were in the way. This was doing nothing to ease the pain in his shoulder. He was supposed to be keeping it in the sling in front of him, not twisted behind him. He debated telling his captors this but, considering they wouldn't tell him simple information like where they were going, decided against it.

They were smooth drivers, he could give them that. Not once was he bumped or jostled. He might not have even been in a moving car at all if his heightened hearing hadn't picked up the hum of the engine.

He thought about how Lucille would react when she learned he'd been kidnapped. Though, given her radio silence with Michel, it was possible she'd been kidnapped first. Maybe wherever he was going, she'd be there. The idea calmed him a bit. She'd know what to do; she always did.

After an endless amount of driving, they arrived. They were, of course, at Michel's mansion, because where else would they be? The trouble had started there, and there the trouble would end. Hopefully.

It seemed odd that, unlike the rest of the hospital, the psychiatric ward was mostly deserted. But seeing as Lucille didn't make a point out of hanging out in psychiatric wards, or hospitals in general, she had no point of comparison. A lone nurse sat at a desk, half asleep over a pile of paperwork. Lucille hurried by, keeping her steps as light as possible. When she was out of sight of the desk, she hissed at Simon, "Which room?"

This time Simon came through right away. "Solitary confinement room B. Apparently she got into a fight with one of the inmates or, uh, patients earlier and they put her in there. Amazing the stuff you can find when you hack into someone's files."

"I thought you said she was admitted today?"

"She was. Stay on your toes. This woman is dangerous."

Lucille ditched the clipboard and followed the arrows to the solitary confinement area. With the way things were going tonight, she expected to find padded cells holding babbling people in straitjackets. Instead they were normal, single-occupant hospital rooms that locked from the outside.

She found B and peered through the small window at the plain, white-walled space beyond. On the twin bed lay a woman in a bikini bottom and a floral hospital gown, snoring. Her blonde hair was plastered to her face, damp and sticking out at odd angles. From this distance, Lucille couldn't tell what age she was. She might have been fifty or fifteen, her plastic surgery was that pervasive.

"We have a problem," she said to her microphone.

"She's not there?"

"No, she's here. She's most certainly here. She's passed out in her room, dead to the world. Because, you know, it's the middle of the night."

"That bitch!"

Lucille contemplated the situation before her. She didn't want to go into the room. She'd been hoping, unrealistically, that she'd find the occupant awake, in an unbarred room, where she could whisper at her from the doorway. No part of her wanted to be trapped with a murderous lunatic supermodel. Given the choice, she'd take Sylvia Stanton any day.

At least Sylvia had only *tried* to murder someone. Beverly Walton had gone through with it.

Gathering all her strength and promises to kill Simon herself if she got out of this alive, Lucille unlocked the door and slipped inside, careful to leave a crack so she could escape.

"Can you wake her up?"

"Probably, if I can figure out how. You don't have a long poking stick in that creepy van of yours, do you?"

"No."

"Fine. Then I'll throw my shoe at her." And she did. She lifted her pant leg, revealing the leather boots she'd been tiptoeing around on for the better part of an hour. Pulling one off, she leaned against the wall beside the door and lobbed it at Beverly's head. The boot hit the back wall and fell right onto Beverly's sleeping face. The model flailed, causing her to fall off the narrow mattress and waking her from her slumber. She gave a bellow and pushed herself off the floor, blinking and glaring through her mess of dirty hair at Lucille.

"What. The. Fuck."

"Yeah, okay, sorry about that." Lucille gave her best apology smile.

Beverly scoffed. She had dark rings of mascara around her eyes and lipstick smeared up to her nose. From this new angle, Lucille put her closer to the fifty range and applauded her plastic surgeon for making her look thirty-five.

"Beverly Walton?"

"Yeah?"

"Oh my God. I'm just such a huge fan of yours!" When they'd discussed it earlier, Lucille and Simon had both agreed she should play the woo girl. It felt weird. Lucille hadn't been a woo girl since high school, but she was a professional.

"You're not a doctor."

Lucille shook her head, smiling as big as she could. "Nope, but they totally bought it. This was the only way I could get to you. No one's seen you in years, and oh my God, I can't believe it's really you."

"Why," Beverly said, grimacing as she pulled herself off the floor and back to her bed, "did you throw your boot at me? Nice knock-offs, by the way."

"They aren't knock-offs. They're originals from your line. I've had them for years and knew I had to wear them when I came to see you!"

"Am I supposed to be flattered that you threw one of my own boots at me?"

Lucille looked contrite. "I really am sorry. It's just...you were sleeping, and I really need to talk to you..."

Lucille waited for Beverly to ask why she hadn't nudged her awake like a normal person. She didn't.

"Can't it wait until tomorrow, when I get out of this hellhole?" Beverly's gaze roamed the empty room, unfocused and incoherent. According to Simon's source, Beverly had laid low for the past eight years but was a regular guest at this particular psych ward, checked in once a month by her eighty-five-year-old mother.

Lucille looked down at her solitary boot. "No."

Beverly gave a huge sigh, leaned back against the wall, and closed her eyes. "Then what?"

Lucille paused long enough for Beverly to open her eyes. Then she glanced out to the empty hallway, like she didn't want this to be overheard. "It's private."

The model rolled her eyes. "There's no one here. They shut all the crazies up and turned out the lights."

"It's about...Simon Anton," Lucille whispered.

The change in Beverly's expression was immediate. Instead of unfocused, detached, and drugged, she looked sober, wide-awake, and very interested. "Oh honey, what'd that fucker do to you?"

Lucille drew back for effect. "What makes you think he did something to me?"

"Because it's what he does. He comes into your life playing fucking Jesus and then slips away when all hell breaks loose." Beverly's jaw clenched. Her face would have turned red in anger, but she didn't seem to have the ability to show emotion any longer.

Lucille looked at Beverly long and hard, sizing her up. Then allowed her shoulders to crumble, in a vulnerable breakdown. "Yeah, he did. He ruined my career, my marriage, my life. Because of him, my sweet twin babies have to...have to...go to public school!"

Beverly inhaled sharply. "No."

Lucille nodded, hiding her face in her hands. "It's true."

"That bastard!" Beverly stood up and started pacing her little room, unsteady on her own bare feet, favoring her left side. "That conniving asshole. That goddamn motherfucker!"

This went on for quite a while, with Lucille fake crying, Beverly running through her repertoire of curse words, and no one coming to check on the commotion. Finally, Beverly sank down on the starched sheets, too exhausted to hold up her own weight anymore. Lucille wiped her dry eyes but let her lip quiver.

"I know you want revenge, honey. I want it too. I almost had it once. But I've been trying to track down that man for eight years with no luck."

"What do you mean?"

Beverly got a long, far-off look on her face. "He disappeared without a trace right after—" She choked, her own fake tears caught in her throat. "But that's a long story."

Lucille's face was intent on Beverly's. In her ear, Simon was listening so hard she could hear him breathing. "I have time."

It was Beverly's turn to eye her up and down. She walked over, picked up the discarded boot from the floor, and handed it to Lucille. "I guess anyone who still has the boots from my collection seven years after they were discontinued has to be trustworthy, right?"

Lucille nodded. She didn't mention that they'd picked the boots up that night from one of Simon's old connections, a costume shop he used to frequent under the name Anton Marcos. They were uncomfortable, a size too small, and the best decision Lucille had made that night was taking the one off to throw at their designer. Now she put it back on, trying to hide her flinch as she zipped it up.

"Simon Anton was arrested eight years ago after my friend and part-time lover Cooper was horribly murdered."

Lucille gasped appropriately. "No. And you think he did it?"

Beverly laughed. It was a cold, empty laugh. "No, but it was his fault."

Lucille shook her head. "I don't understand."

Beverly sighed. "I told you it was a long story. Let me go back. I met Cooper one night at a party. One of those parties where everyone has already fucked everyone else and is just waiting for the right moment to release nude pics on the Internet, you know?"

Lucille would like to say she didn't know, but she'd worked in this town for too long and had cleaned up after more than a few of those parties. So she nodded.

"Then there was Cooper. No one knew who he was. He just kinda appeared there—rich guy, houses all over the place, gorgeous as sin, and completely untouchable, unless you were one of the select few to be invited to one of his weekend getaways. He was all over me that night, flirting with me, eye fucking me across the bar, you know how it is."

This time Lucille could definitely say she didn't. Not out loud, of course.

"He said he'd seen some of my early work, this really obscure nude shoot I did for a BDSM magazine when I was younger. I couldn't believe it. He said that if I was actually into that stuff and wanted to explore more ways to unleash my sexuality, to come to his house party that weekend. Obviously, I went. No one turned down Cooper. It was...erotic, deeply, deeply erotic." Beverly trailed off, leaning against the wall with a sigh and a shiver. "Mmm. You see, Cooper chose only the best. And I mean the best everything, you know?"

*Again, no idea.*

"This one weekend was different. Someone suggested a change to the...routine. Cooper was angry about the suggestion, but we eventually swayed him to our side. Perhaps it did go a little too far," she mused. "Cooper was going on and on about overstepping the boundaries between the sacred and the profane, but I was like, what the fuck have we been doing this whole time?

"Whatever. Things got out of control and someone died. It was one of our group members who was great to look at but kind of a bore to talk to. The whole thing was a total accident, of course. I couldn't even tell you what happened anymore. One moment he was alive and humping the shit out of a dude chained to the wall, and the next moment he was dead and covered in blood.

"It was, like, all a blur after that. Cooper flipped out because it was all on camera."

Lucille gasped, for real this time. *What is wrong with her? Why is she telling me all of this?* Because there was something wrong, something very wrong with Beverly. She spoke like she was reciting a monologue, without emotional investment in her words.

Beverly didn't even blink. "Oh yes, we recorded all our...experiments. Kept us going until we got together the next time, you know? But this was, like, really on video. Right front and center on video. You could see faces. Fuck, my face all over it. And not just my face; other parts, too.

"Anyway, Cooper freaked out, kicked us out, and kept the tape for himself. He kept going on and on about murder. But it wasn't a murder, you know? Because it was a total accident. We all tried to tell Cooper that it was an accident, we could just explain that to the police, and then it'd all be over. But

Cooper said they wouldn't understand, they'd find the tape anyway, so we might as well turn ourselves in now. We tried to get Anton to talk him down, but the fucker said he only dealt with PR issues for his clients, not criminal activity. PR issues, my ass. He was at more than a few of those parties."

Lucille did not want to hear that about her uncle. Of course, it did clarify a lot of things about her adolescence, like when Simon had showed her how to tie a bondage rope on her fourteenth birthday. Still, he was her uncle.

When his name came up, the fucker in question gasped in her ear. She ignored him. "Do you think Anton was trying to get Cooper to go to the police?"

Beverly nodded. "Uh huh. Even though he joined in, he was always aloof, you know? Like he was too good for us."

Lucille could hear Simon itching to protest and begged him to keep silent. This changed things. It made sense her uncle would encourage Cooper to take the video to the police. Cooper would come across as a hero for trying to save his friends from sexual deviancy and, in the process, save himself.

Beverly brought the attention back to herself with a dramatic wave of her hand. "Whatever. It didn't matter after a while. I stopped sleeping and eating as a result of the stress. Every moment I expected the police to show up at my door or my agent to call and say the video had leaked. I looked awful. Though you'd think modeling agencies would want someone skinny who worked late hours to avoid going home. They did, but apparently they didn't want a model who twitched all the time and looked like a startled chipmunk. They dropped me. Everyone dropped me. Not even the fucking plastic surgery helped."

For a moment, Lucille felt for the half-naked former model. It was brief, and then she returned to her loathing. Heartwarming anecdote or no, this woman was the key to getting Simon's name cleared, and Lucille needed her to say the magic words.

"I blamed Anton, of course. If it had only been Cooper, we could have talked him down, but the little shit was protecting him. So I decided to sneak into his house, get one of his guns, and make it look like a suicide."

Lucille started. There was a rustling in her ear and then silence.

"But Cooper was there too. I couldn't figure out why, because they were mumbling away in these low voices that I couldn't understand or whatever. But, I couldn't have a witness, obviously, so I left. The next day Anton was arrested for Cooper's murder, and I figured he'd got what was coming to him."

"That was the night Cooper was murdered?" Lucille gasped with the appropriate stunned, wide-eyed gaze.

Beverly smiled. It was scary. "Uh huh. Bullet to the chest, that very night."

"Wasn't Anton arrested for it?"

Beverly laughed her empty cackle. "Son of a bitch escaped. I don't know how, but he got out. There was a rumor his little niece helped him, but I think it was some of his other 'clients.'"

Lucille swallowed at the mention of herself. She would've helped Simon escape if she hadn't been left in the dark. All she'd done was break up with the boyfriend who'd turned her only stable family member in in the first place.

"So Anton murdered Cooper, and now we're going to murder Anton as revenge."

Beverly studied Lucille for a long minute, her eyes once again unfocused. "No. The police think Anton murdered Cooper, but I never thought he did."

"Because you killed Cooper."

"What did you say?" Beverly moved toward Lucille, stumbling.

*Oops.* Lucille scrambled. "Oh, I'm so sorry. I didn't mean to assume. You'd never... I mean, you couldn't..."

Beverly stopped, her face blank. "No, you're right, aren't you? I mean, I did, didn't I? I killed him."

There it was. The confession. A little wishy washy, and probably enough to get her off on an insanity plea, but it would be able to clear Simon. All Lucille had to do was extract herself from the situation and they were home free.

At that moment, five feet and ten inches of gay man dressed in a false beard and a pair of wire-rimmed spectacles appeared in the room beside her. From beneath the folds of his black overcoat peeked the business end of a pistol, pointed directly at Beverly's fake boobs.

# Chapter Twenty-One

"Anton!" Beverly screeched in a decibel meant only for dogs.

"What the hell are you doing here?" Lucille hissed. "I've got it under control."

"Sorry, darling, I couldn't waste the opportunity," Simon said, not looking away from Beverly. His eyes narrowed, his jaw clenched, and the brown fake beard quivered.

"Darling?" Beverly cursed. She was hyperventilating and getting louder by the second. Simon twitched the gun, and Beverly shut up and backed against the wall, shaking. "You tricked me! You lying, sneaking little bitch," she whisper-hissed.

Simon spoke, his voice low and dangerous. "I could do it, you know. I could pull this trigger right here, right now."

Beverly folded her arms, her jaw clenched. "Fine. Do it."

Simon stared at her and she back at him, a deadly game of chicken.

Lucille glared at both of them, but they didn't notice. "What are you doing here?" she asked her uncle again. "We've got the confession—just hand it over and be done with it."

Beverly growled. "You were recording me?"

Lucille rolled her eyes at the hot mess in the corner. "Keep up." She turned back to Simon.

"Yes, right, confession. Good job, Lucy. You can go now." His eyes didn't leave Beverly's face.

"You can't kill her, you know."

Simon blinked then and looked at her. "What?"

"You can't kill her. First of all, there are too many witnesses. Second of all, there are security guards who will definitely hear the gunshot. I just got you back from being on the run. If you act like a stupid ass and kill her now, I'll lose you all over again."

"Who said anything about killing her? I came in to get the recording from you and bring it to the police now, before they release her and she has a chance to run."

Lucille didn't believe him. "Good. But you can see how I got confused, right? What with you standing here in a ridiculous disguise and a gun poking out of your coat?"

"Don't worry so much, Lucy. It causes wrinkles."

Lucille snorted. "You're impossible."

Beverly had moved closer to them, listening to every word. "Told you you couldn't do it, Anton. You always were a pussy."

"Don't listen to her. She's like a word-vomit volcano of TMI."

Simon shrugged. "Eh, I've been called worse. Now will you get out of here? If things go wrong and I do get arrested, I want to make sure you're gone."

Lucille frowned. "What do you mean if things go wrong?"

"Lucy, we're standing in a psychiatric ward at a well-populated hospital where I, a fugitive from the law in a ridiculous disguise, am holding a gun to a former model's fake rack. There is any number of ways things could go wrong. Such as standing around talking instead of moving. Got it?"

"Got it." She gave him a sideways hug and a kiss on the cheek for good luck. Then she turned and waved to Beverly. "It was interesting meeting you, Beverly. Have fun in prison!"

"Bite me."

"A real charmer, that one." Lucille grinned as she tottered out on her stupid, pinching boots. She was going to burn them when she got home.

They were fucked. Here they were, held against their will by his crazy, tiny cousin who had his best friend's balls in a vise. Not to mention her enormous, mobster-looking henchmen, of which there were two in this room. Brett recognized them; they worked for Stanton security, the private, highly trained personal guard of the Stanton dynasty. These were men who followed orders no matter what. Even when those orders came from a deranged attempted murderess who really should not be in charge, considering she was holding two innocent men's lives at stake and trying to force one of them to marry her.

Brett struggled with his bonds, his hand brushing against something in his back pocket. His cell phone. Conniving, manipulative, and bitchy were all great adjectives to describe his cousin. Brilliant, she was not.

Brett somehow got the thing unlocked. *Stupid touch screens.* He hoped none of the burly henchmen were watching him since it looked like he was itching his butt. Their attention, however, was trained on their boss, who was in the middle of some complex mating ritual wherein she alterna-tively tried to woo Michel and junk punch him. They were smirking.

He probed the screen until the slight buzz told him he'd hit a phone number and was calling some-one. *Please let it not be Michel,* he thought, *please let it not be Michel.* Luckily, Sylvia started screaming at Michel just then. It covered up the sound of Lucille answering.

The way out was far easier than the way in. No one stopped her or looked her way as she hurried through the halls. *Please let Simon not do something stupid,* she chanted in time to her footsteps.

Outside, she turned her phone back on. It rang. *Scary,* she thought as she headed to her car. It was Brett. Lucille debated answering. She didn't want to get into anything with Brett, at least not anything of the talking-about-feelings variety. She was on a high from the undercover work. She could see why there was so much sex in James Bond movies. All that stealth and subterfuge made a girl horny. And even though Brett claimed to want more and the sex hadn't been that mind-blowing, she couldn't think of anyone else she'd rather bang right at that moment.

"Hey there, hot stuff."

Only before she could tell him to meet her at her place in twenty minutes, there was loud static and then a woman's voice.

"You don't think I'd do it, do you? You don't think I'd kill you? You sadly underestimate what I'm capable of," said the voice. It sounded familiar. The phone cut out.

*Sylvia Stanton.*

Lucille sprinted the rest of the way to her car. Sometime between the tête-á-tête at her house and now, all hell had broken loose. *Send a boy to do a woman's job,* she thought bitterly.

Her mind raced. She had no idea where they were, only that Brett, Michel, and Sylvia were together and one of them would soon be dead. Simon probably had phone-tracing equipment in the creepy van he'd brought for their hospital break-in. But even if she had the equipment, she didn't know how to use it and she couldn't ask Simon due to the whole Beverly situation. If she alerted the police, Sylvia would off both men before the first siren finished wailing. The heiress sounded desperate and insane enough that Lucille had no doubt she'd follow through on her threat to kill.

There was no time to contemplate motive or intent. Lucille needed to find them now. She decided to start at the most likely place and work from there.

Brett didn't know whether Lucille had gotten the call. She'd answered and said something provocative at him, so that was a promising beginning. But then Sylvia had got right in his face, like inches away from his nose. He jumped as far as the ropes binding him would allow, enough to come down on his cell phone. He heard a crunch as the screen broke and the phone cut out. They were well and truly on their own.

His shoulder ached. It was stretched behind his back at an odd angle, the sling lying discarded on the floor beside him. After everything that had happened that day, all the sleep and the sex and the arguments, his arm told him it couldn't take much more. But there was nothing he could do—he was being held hostage by a tiny blonde nightmare.

They were in Michel's "artist" room on the third floor. Brett had been there once before, when Michel had first moved in and the man had still invited him over for dinner and brainstorming. It was a small room in comparison to the rest of the house, boxy, with only one window high above the antique Persian rug. The space was covered in musical instruments, books, scraps of paper, and eclectic furniture that in no way fit the other home décor. The chair Brett was tied to, for instance, looked like something his niece would bring home from a furniture painting class, if he had a niece and she did that sort of thing. The one Michel was in was deep burgundy and leather, the type of chair an early nineteenth-century gentleman would lounge in while his valet brought him port and a cigar. Brett could only imagine the pain Michel's arms were in, strapped around the wide middle of the chair, his ankles lashed to each leg. If Brett didn't know better, he'd have said Michel was prepping for a kinky sex scene. All that was missing were some nipple clamps and a ball gag.

The traitorous security guards were starting to fidget. Brett understood. Sylvia tended to monologue when she thought someone was listening, and here she had two unwilling and unmoving participants. Judging by the tone of her voice, she wasn't happy with her fiancé about something and was making a big deal over it.

"I just don't get it!" she yelled, waving her arms around as she spoke. She'd always been abnormally loud. "Why, Michel? Why?"

Michel looked confused. And dazed. It could have had something to do with the fact she'd kneed him in the gut a minute ago or the drugs Sylvia had used to get them to the third floor without a struggle or any number of reasons, none of which had to do with his ranting, murderous fiancée. Somehow, Brett thought none of those were it and that the expression had everything to do with said woman.

"Why what, my sweet?"

Sylvia scowled. "Don't give me that. You know exactly what I'm talking about."

Michel didn't. None of them did. When Michel didn't answer, Sylvia let out a frustrated screech and began wandering around the room.

"I hate this room. I've always hated this room. That's why you kept it, didn't you? Because you knew I hated it and you just wanted to piss me off. Look at all this crap. Do you think I can take people on a tour of the house and risk them seeing this dump? No. But does Michel Polce, world-class asshole, care about that? No."

It was getting boring. She hadn't told them why they were there, except that Brett was an ordained minister. Yeah, ordained online by the Church of America for the low cost of thirty bucks. One of those stupid, drunken mistakes. He wondered how Sylvia had even found out about it.

Did Lucille make stupid drunken mistakes? Doubtful. She was always in control, always so put together. Except, of course, when he annoyed her and her eyebrow started to twitch and, next thing he knew, she was dragging him off somewhere to make out with him and then violently injure him again. Or when she gave that little sound and arched her back when he touched her the way she liked. That wasn't controlled at all.

Still, he wondered why she'd put up with all of his drunken escapades. Then he stopped. She hadn't. He hadn't had any drunken escapades since he'd met her. Not since the night they'd met, in fact, and he'd realized he needed to be on his game around this woman. He'd been drinking, but not alone. He'd been with people, drinking socially. Talking, having fun, laughing, scared shitless, and in pain, like he was now, but he'd been there and remembered all of it.

Well, except when he'd passed out or been knocked out, neither of which were his fault.

Sylvia had stopped talking and was staring at him.

"What?"

"Were you listening at all?"

"No."

She growled again. "I said, you're going to marry us now."

"Me and you? Gross. We're related."

She stalked over and slapped him, nearly dislocating his jaw.

"No, dumbass. Marry Michel and me so I can get on to the killing-you bit."

# Chapter Twenty-Two

L ucille ditched her car a few blocks from Michel's mansion. She hoped to God they were there. In the two days she'd known Michel, they for some reason hadn't discussed his favorite haunts. If she had to search the city or fly commercial back to Mino, they'd be dead before she arrived.

Her stomach lurched at the thought. In all her cases over the years, all the mayhem and fucked-up situations, she'd never been close to losing a client. Not to death, anyway. Now she stood to lose not only the first client she'd ever walked away from, but also the man she had weird and confusing feelings for.

She crept along the hedge toward the house. Thank God for rich socialites and their fascination with tall hedges.

At his gate, she peered down the long driveway, straining to see any sign of movement at the end.

Here, however, the whims of the rich and famous foiled her. The street lamps, neon signs, and other various lights that kept the rest of the city at a bright, hazy glow even at one o'clock in the morning were entirely absent from Michel's street. There was a light on in the upper part of the house and another in the area she thought was the summer kitchen, where she'd agreed to have sex with Matt in exchange for his silence not three days earlier. How much had changed in so short a time. As it was, she would give anything for Matt's presence right now. Sure, the police would make a lot of noise and Matt would give her part four of his speech about how they were meant to be together, but at least the lights from the squad cars would cut through all this black nothingness.

Lucille debated the validity of her previous thoughts when she saw movement. A shape crossed in front of the weak light from the back of the house. In the near silence, she heard a car door open, and in the light from inside the car, she saw the outline of a massive figure. A voice from a second someone called to the person in the car in a loud hiss. It was a deep voice, even whispering. No doubt belonging to another huge, muscular guy. Sylvia didn't travel light, that was certain. Even though she'd felt like

Lara Croft at the hospital, Lucille wasn't about to take on Sylvia's goons.

Her phone buzzed and she jumped, coming down awkwardly on her foot. *Shit, fucking shitty shit shit!* She pulled the phone out and silenced it, her fingers shaking and her foot smarting from the landing. Some secret agent she was.

*Speak of the devil and he shall call,* she thought when she saw Matt's name flash across the screen. If he'd blown her cover with that call, she'd kill him. It would be the far less graceful way of getting out of the celebrity spin doctor business, but in a pinch, it'd work.

Lucille listened for signs that the men had heard the vibrating phone. The car door closed and their voices moved away from her, toward the back of the house. She let out her held breath and changed Matt's name in her phone to "fucking asshole." Childish, perhaps, but it gave her a small comfort as she set about scaling the ten-foot-high hedge in a rustling, graceless manner.

If any guards were still out front, they would have heard the commotion. By the time she dropped into the tree-lined drive leading to the mansion, her hands smarting from the poky branches, her clothes covered in leaves and dirt, she was convinced they'd all retreated indoors. Luck, it seemed, was temporarily on her side.

Lucille hadn't noticed on her previous visits, given she'd been driving and in kind of a hurry both times, but Michel's front lawn was annoyingly devoid of cover. Across the lush green expanse of grass there were a few ornamental shrubs, a couple of twisting, tiny trees, a few flower beds that helped no one with anything, and not much else. Just picturesque, well-kept grass that stretched on along the grand driveway. She had never been so frustrated by a well-manicured lawn in her life. True, she'd also never been trying to break into a house in her life and, therefore, hadn't yet dealt with the challenges presented by landscaping. There may not have been a guard out front, but she wasn't taking any chances. She crept from tiny shrub to tiny tree, feeling like an idiot. All she needed was to start singing her own theme music and she'd be an ideal candidate for the mental ward, if she wasn't already.

After an eternity of sneaking across the lawn, Lucille reached the house. She saw why the front was unguarded—there were security cameras everywhere. She should have known Michel would have the place under constant surveillance. There was but a slim chance they hadn't seen her dance across the yard. Though if someone was watching, she kind of hoped they'd kill her now and save her the shame.

She stood against the side of the house, her black boots soaked in the dew from the grass, her scrubs smeared brown and green, feeling way out of her league, waiting to die. If it were only Michel inside, she'd say screw it. He'd gotten himself into this shit show and he could damn well get himself out of it. She'd already quit and stormed off. But the fact that Brett was there, too—that changed things. Brett, who she liked but couldn't stand. If he were killed before she told him that, she'd never forgive herself. That, despite the potential for public mockery and death, was why she was still there.

No one came.

Lucille sighed and pushed away from the adobe wall of the house. There were only two places the hostages could be: the summer kitchen or the third-floor room with the light. She'd try the kitchen first; it was closer.

She crept around the side of the house, scraping her hands more than a few times on the rough walls. *Damn Michel and his expensive adobe villa. If we all come out of this alive, I'll kill him myself.*

As she neared the summer kitchen, she crouched down to avoid being seen through the screen walls

of the porch. There was, of course, a hedge row below the windows, and she crawled along this, hoping
the shadows of the bushes were enough to cover
her. From inside the kitchen she heard voices.

"Someone has to go deal with it," said a low man's
voice.

"I think it's a she," replied another male voice,
higher pitched but gravely.

"Who cares if it's a she? It's a potential threat," the
first replied.

Lucille froze. They were talking about her. Which
meant they'd seen her on the cameras. Her blood
rushed in her ears as her heart threatened to burst
through her chest in wild panic.

A door opened. "Still nothing on the cameras. I
don't know what she wants us looking for, because
whatever it is, it isn't there." A new voice said this,
another man.

"She's paranoid."

The first man spoke again. "I really think we
should do something about the tiger."

The new guy answered. "Is that some kind of a
code word?"

"No. It's a real, fucking tiger. This rich bastard has
a goddamn fucking tiger."

"Jesus. Where?"

"It has a habitat at the back of the property. I'd hate to be here if the power ever went out. Could have a real fucking *Jurassic Park* situation on our hands." It was the first man again, his voice rising as he began to panic.

Lucille couldn't believe what she was hearing. Of course Michel had a tiger. Because why wouldn't he? When you have millions of dollars and no boundaries, why not get a tiger and build an illegal habitat for it on your property? This explained why the guards had missed her less-than-stealthy entrance, and for that she was grateful to Michel. Maybe she wouldn't kill him, just cut him out of her life like a frost-bitten limb.

"That explains the tranq gun."

"I'm not taking chances."

"Okay, Rambo. Roy, get back to your perimeter sweep. Lark and I will stay on the cameras until we get an update from the boss. I'd hoped to have this over and done by now. I don't know what she's waiting for. Every minute we're here we run the risk that one of those nut jobs will get free and call the cops."

"I'll guard that tiger."

"Sure, you do that."

*That guy has some weird fascination with the tiger. Whatever. One less to deal with.*

The door opened and closed again. Then a door much closer to her opened. The outside door. The two men were coming her way. Lucille scrambled around the side of the house, out of sight.

As soon as she couldn't hear the men anymore, she crept back to the summer kitchen. They'd left the inside door open and the screen door unlocked. It took less than two seconds to slip into the room. The room that was blazing with light. Still, it was safer than being caught outside by the tiger-ob-sessed guy with the tranquilizer gun or the other guy who, although he seemed more rational, was no doubt toting a real gun.

Lucille slipped into the dark living room and crashed right into a wall of man. The third man, the one who was supposed to be back in the surveil-lance room, had not listened to his own orders and was standing in the pitch-black sitting room.

Lucille's first thought was that she had the el-ement of surprise on her side. Her second was a realization that he had also surprised her and she wasn't carrying a weapon. The third was that he was at least a head taller than her and far more muscular, the kind of muscular that could break her arm with his bare hands. The fourth thought was an observation that he was holding a glass of whiskey in one hand and a decanter in the other.

She acted on an instinct not her own. Before the guy could so much as say, "Who the fuck are you?" she kneed him in the groin. It was a long way up to his groin, given his height, and she felt a strain in her muscles that she'd pay for tomorrow, but she got a good smack in.

"What the fuck?" the man said as he doubled over.

Lucille grabbed his shoulders and kneed him again because she didn't know what else to do. The man fell to the floor, dropping the glass and de-canter as he fell in order to grasp his throbbing nether regions.

"Who the fuck are you?" he gasped as he struggled to stand back up.

Lucille wanted to have a quippy line ready. Some-thing about her being his worst nightmare or a mes-sage for his boss or some other bad-ass nonsense. She had nothing. So she shrugged, picked up the decanter, and smashed it over the man's head.

Glass and whiskey went everywhere. She cut her finger on a piece. But the man went unconscious, his hands still resting on his crotch. She looked down at him, sucking on her bleeding finger. He was covered in something wet, and she didn't think it was all whiskey. If a piece of glass had gotten lodged in his brain and he died, she'd feel really bad. She hadn't thought the decanter fragile enough to shatter like that, so this could all be seen as one giant, horrible accident.

"Um, sorry," she said to him. "I had no idea that was going to be so bloody."

*Maybe I should write him an apology note for when he wakes up. What? No. I'm Lucille fucking Anton. I don't write apology notes. Besides, paper trail.*

She did check to see if he was breathing. He was. She left.

The rest of her trip to the third floor was unimpeded by lurking men. She had no idea where Michel's surveillance room was, but it didn't seem to be between her and the target, so she put it out of her mind. There were other things to think about, such as what she was going to do when she walked in on Sylvia and the hostages. She didn't have a gun or a plan. She was wearing dirty, smelly clothes, her hair was a mess, and her thighs burned from the unaccustomed crouching. She had no idea what she'd find. Well, except Sylvia, Brett, Michel, and more guards with guns.

As Lucille crossed the second-floor landing and made her way to the spiral staircase that led to the third floor, an idea struck her.

Two minutes later, hair brushed, face washed, wearing one of Sylvia's bombshell dresses and heels, Lucille knocked on the third-floor door.

"Michel? Are you in here?" she asked as she opened the door and walked into the mayhem within.

# CHAPTER TWENTY-THREE

From his vantage point, tied to the chair behind Michel's enormous mahogany desk, Brett gaped as Lucille waltzed into the room, wearing a body-hugging, low-cut navy dress with a side slit up to the thigh. His mouth went dry from being open for so long. She was walking into what he knew she knew was a hostage situation led by a mad woman with a gun, without cops or her uncle or a weapon of any kind other than that dress. But wow, that dress.

*This is no time to get an erection,* he told himself sternly.

No one moved for a long minute. Lucille started to back out of the room, with a sheepish expression. "Oh. It looks like you're in the middle of something. I won't interrupt your kinky sex thing."

Sylvia recovered first. "Who the fuck are you?"

Her voice screeched. Even lovesick Michel couldn't still be smitten with her after listening to that for the past two hours. Then again, Michel had been listening to that voice for years and was still head over heels. They were toast.

"Sorry, I just came to see Michel about a business thing. I'll come back at a better time."

Sylvia, when startled by the sudden arrival, had whipped her gun around to Lucille instead of Michel. Her face was orange-red under her tan. She sputtered with anger and motioned wildly with the gun. "Grab her," she squeaked at her guards.

Two of the henchmen took hold of Lucille and pulled her into the room, her arms behind her back.

"Put her over there." Sylvia motioned to the armchair next to Michel.

The guards plunked Lucille into the armchair, almost causing her boobs to pop out of the dress. A *pity*, Brett thought. Anger replaced chagrin. There was no way in hell these douchebags—he included Michel in that—were going to see the woman he definitely, probably liked's boobs.

They tied her arms behind the chair as Lucille asked, in her best innocent voice, "Michel, what's going on here?"

Michel, who this whole time had been looking varying degrees of contrite, amped it up a level as he turned to his spin doctor. "I'm sorry to drag you into all this, Lucille. I didn't know we had a meeting scheduled or I would have canceled it. Of course, I also didn't know Sylvia would be here tonight. It seems I'm out of the loop on a lot of things."

"It's okay, I understand, Michel." Lucille leaned over as best she could to bump shoulders with him.

Brett glared at both of them. From his periphery, he saw Sylvia advancing on Lucille.

"Shut up," she said, her voice a growl. "I want to know who you are, how the fuck you got past my guards, what the fuck you think you're doing with my fiancé, and why the fuck you're wearing my dress!"

There was silence as Lucille held Sylvia's blazing gaze but said nothing.

Brett smirked. Lucille was wearing Sylvia's dress. Ingenious. Of course his fashion-crazed cousin would recognize her own clothes. And of course nothing would make her angrier than seeing them on someone she assumed was her rival for Michel's love. If Lucille's plan also included a way of getting them out of this mess, they'd be all set.

"Can I speak?" Lucille asked politely.

"You'd better before I shoot your brains out." Sylvia's own black tank and pants were wrinkled, her black makeup heavy, and her tan patchy. Beside the radiant, well-rested Lucille, Sylvia was a mess, the strain of the past few days glaring in contrast with her composed captive. It had to be driving Sylvia insane. Her hand shook and her jaw clenched with barely suppressed rage.

"Oh, because you told me to shut up. Just wanted to clarify that you actually do want me to talk." Lucille's face was calm as she spoke, not giving away any indication she was scared of the starlet before her.

If Brett thought that dress was going to give him a boner, the sight of her playing it cool was enough to send him over the edge. He could picture this as a sex game they played, tying each other up, acting calm in the face of danger, but really getting hot and bothered and throwing around dirty phrases and slow strip teases.

Right when Brett started feeling like he needed a cold shower, Sylvia went and ruined it. She let out a growl and pointed the gun right at Lucille's head. Lucille didn't flinch, but the action was enough to snap Brett back to the real and present danger. After the last few hours, he had no doubt that Sylvia would never be able to kill Michel in cold blood. Lucille, though, meant nothing to her. Sylvia might be far enough gone to go through with it.

"You don't want to do that," Lucille said, her eyes on Sylvia's. "There are way too many witnesses."

"Witnesses who will be dead," Sylvia hissed back.

Lucille frowned a little, a confused frown like she was trying to work it all out. "Okay, right. You want to kill Michel. And Brett for some reason. Actually, what is that reason? Why are you doing this?"

Sylvia's lips were pressed in a thin line. She looked like she was considering spitting on Lucille. Instead she said, "You first. Why the fuck are you at my fiancé's house in the middle of the night, wearing my fucking dress, and how the fuck did you get in here?"

"Fine, I'll start. I got a booty call from Brett a bit ago—we're hooking up, you see—but he didn't say where he was. I came over to see if Michel knew. But no one was answering the gate so I had to climb over the hedge, ripping my own dress in the process. I didn't think it'd be appropriate to show up to talk to my lover's best friend wearing a dress ripped up to my vagina, so I borrowed one of yours. I had no idea you were holding these guys hostage in here or I'd never have presumed—"

Sylvia cut her off with another growl. "Shut up. That is the dumbest story I've ever heard in my life." She cocked the gun.

Lucille gave Sylvia a look like she wanted to say something but didn't want to at the same time.

"What? It'd better be good, because it's the last thing you'll ever say."

Lucille sighed dramatically. "It's just that I was going to dry clean this dress before I gave it back to you, but blood stains are really hard to get out, and also I'd have a hard time footing the bill, since I'd be dead and all."

Brett looked from one woman to the other. He saw the guards doing the same, both of them ready to spring the moment their boss gave the word. Michel wasn't paying attention, though. His face was twisted like he was in pain, his brow frowned in concentration. In fact, he didn't seem to be aware there was anything else happening in the room, let alone a life-or-death standoff.

"Who cares? It's just a dress," Sylvia said through gritted teeth, her voice catching on the words.

"Just a dress? Just a dress?" Lucille repeated. "This is a $56,000 dress designed personally for you by Martín Piero himself. I'd say it's a little more than just a dress."

Another heart-stopping moment, the tension so palpable it zinged through the room. Then Sylvia lowered the gun.

Brett let out the breath he hadn't realized he was holding. If he wasn't tied to a chair, he'd have kissed Lucille right then and there, in front of everyone. True, she hadn't figured out how to get them out of the situation yet. Sylvia still had the gun, they were still tied up, and there were still a shit ton of highly trained guards surrounding the house. But that dress move was brilliant. If they made it out of here alive, he wasn't going to waste any time in ripping it off of her, bystanders be damned.

"I hate you." Sylvia scowled. "I don't know who you are, but I hate you."

"I'm sorry, I'm Lucille. It's nice to finally meet you." Lucille gave her a big smile.

"I can't say the same."

Lucille nodded. "That's understandable. Now, there's something I still don't get, though. Why are you trying to kill Michel?"

All eyes—save, once again, Michel's—were trained on Sylvia. It was the question they'd all been wondering, guards and hostages alike.

"For his money, duh." Sylvia looked at them all like they were stupid.

"But isn't your father one of the richest men in the world?"

Sylvia's look didn't change. "Where have you been? In Saudi Arabia with your head up your ass? My father cut me off six months ago. Some bullshit about not amounting to anything while living off his money."

Brett spoke up. He'd, after all, almost died, on multiple occasions, for his curiosity on this particular subject, and since death was still an impending option, he might as well get some answers first. "So why try to kill Michel?"

Sylvia turned her how-stupid-are-you look on him. "Duh, he put me in his will? After he dies, I get everything."

Brett nodded. "Thus the accidents..."

"...so no one would accuse you of murder since you're the one with the most to lose," Lucille finished for him.

They locked eyes for a moment and smiled. His last smile from her before they, or at least he, was murdered by a money-crazed bitch.

"Obviously. Only this asshole here"—she motioned to Michel, who snapped out of whatever fantasy land he was in and looked at her in surprise and then looked at Lucille, his face in a crushed, soul-wrenching droop—"added a condition that we had to be married first. So I tried doing the damsel-in-distress thing, only that didn't work because some other asshole who was supposed to give you a lead on where I was decided to blow up the hotel instead. My only option was to kidnap my fiancé and my dumb ordained cousin here, get married, and then kill them both and make it look like a murder/suicide/lover's quarrel."

Michel watched Sylvia with his huge, sad, brown eyes. He looked ready to cry at any moment.

"That may be the most stupidly brilliant plan I've ever heard," Brett said with real awe. She, the greedy ditz willing to do anything to preserve her five-star lifestyle, had played Michel good. Unless something drastic happened, they were, in the simplest sense of the word, fucked.

Lucille sent him a look that said, "Don't encourage her."

A radio crackled. One of the henchmen spoke up. "Miss Stanton, we have a situation downstairs."

Sylvia's rage amped up a level. "What now? Don't tell me one of you called the cops or I'll kill you now and sign the marriage license with your cold, dead hand."

Lucille gave her another sheepish look. "Actually, that might have been me, but I didn't call the cops. I was surprised by one of your guys on my way up, and I may have smashed him over the head with an unnecessarily fragile decanter. One of you should go check that out. He's going to need medical attention."

Both men looked at Sylvia, worried but waiting for permission.

"Well, go already!"

They both made to leave the room.

"Not both of you!"

One of them left, leaving the three tied captives with only Sylvia and one guard in the room. At least Brett thought they were three tied captives.

After the door closed, but before Sylvia turned her attention back to her victims, Michel, somehow untied, sprang from his chair and tackled her, throwing her to the ground and reaching around to grab the gun from her hands.

The guard made to help his boss, but Lucille, too, stood up from her chair, hands unbound, and kneed him hard in the balls.

Brett had to be honest with himself as he watched his best friend and his new whatever fight: he felt a little left out that they hadn't untied him too. The two of them had obviously been plotting since Lucille entered the room, but they hadn't thought to let him in on it. Rude.

He dismissed the jealousy and replaced it with concern. Short-lived concern. Both battles seemed to be going well.

The gun went off. A bullet embedded itself in the chair leg beside Brett's right foot. "Hey, watch it!" he said to no one in particular.

The gun followed shortly after, skidding across the floor to crash into the chair leg by his other foot.

Michel had Sylvia pinned to the floor, but she was attacking him, thrashing her legs to kick him, straining her head up to bite him, her long nails curling to dig into his skin. Michel looked down at her sadly. "I'm sorry, baby," he said. "I should have realized this a long time ago, but it's not going to work out between us."

"Get off of me, you fucking bastard!"

"I just don't think you ever really loved me," Michel went on, oblivious to the venom being spit at him.

Lucille, meanwhile, had kneed the guy a second and third time in the junk and then hit him over the head with a copy of *Michel Polce: An Unauthorized Biography* that Michel had on display nearby. The man fell to the floor with a grunt and didn't get up. A small trickle of blood spilled down his face and onto the hardwood floor.

"Jesus, Lucille," Brett breathed.

"I know," she said. "I didn't need to hit him so hard. It was a little overkill."

Brett shook his head. "It was hot."

Lucille looked at him sternly. "Brett, a man very possibly might have died just now, and you're thinking about sex?"

Brett nodded.

"God, I love you."

Brett froze. He'd been about to quip back, to tell her to come over and untie him so they could screw on Michel's desk. It died in his throat.

Lucille didn't seem to notice what she'd said. She leaned down, checked that the man was breathing, and then walked over to where Michel was pontificating to a feral Sylvia.

Brett had so many comeback lines. *You can't just say that and walk away. I love you too. Untie me so I can kiss you. Let's get out of here. You are my one and only, and I've never loved anyone as much as I do you.* Those were the best of the lot, but none of them were right. His throat closed off and he gaped, fish-like, tied to Michel's desk chair with his numb, injured arm and the clothes he'd been wearing when they'd had sex earlier that day.

Lucille convinced Michel to let Sylvia up and to tie her to a chair.

"Just you wait until my men come back. You may think you're all that, but can you take down five of them at once?" Sylvia was shouting, no doubt trying to be heard by her army downstairs.

Lucille sighed. She walked over, picked up the gun from beside Brett's chair, gave him a wink that made his confusion worse, strolled back, and pointed the gun at Sylvia's head. "I think it's time you stopped talking. We'll take it from here, thanks."

"Lucille, what are you doing?" Michel asked. He stood beside Lucille, looking down at his former fiancée.

"Oh, I'm sorry, would you like to do this?"

Michel nodded. "Kind of, yeah."

Lucille didn't get a chance to hand over the gun. The door flew open, in charged a couple of guys in police uniform, there was a lot of shouting about no one moving, and chaos ensued. A gun went off. Sylvia screamed. Lucille dropped the one she'd been holding as a red stain began to spread from her right shoulder.

# CHAPTER TWENTY-FOUR

Lucille had never been shot before. Of all the stupid, crazy-assed things that had happened in her life, which was now, annoyingly, flashing before her eyes, she'd never once been shot. It wasn't pleasant. She heard the ear-shattering bang when the gun went off and the clatter as the weapon she held fell to the floor. She felt something hit her between those sounds. Then she felt nothing. Someone screamed, and it didn't seem to be her. Her lips were gripped together, her teeth biting into the side of her cheek. Then the pain started. It ripped through her shoulder in an angry, vicious surge. She tasted blood in her mouth and smelled it on her skin. She felt that same blood rushing around inside her, pouring from the open wound, trickling from her bit cheek, rushing in her ears. And the pain. The pain was every kind of torment she'd ever felt and it was all of them at once.

There were a lot of voices, a lot of people saying a lot of things at her. She couldn't sort them out; time wasn't going at its usual speed. Then, in a rush, all the voices came closer, time caught up, and she looked over at her right shoulder and nearly passed out at the sight of the blood, her blood, running down her skin. She swore, adding her enraged agony to the cacophony of madness.

The voices were sorting themselves out now.

"Take it off! Take it off right now before another drop of blood gets on it. I'm serious!" Sylvia was shouting.

Michel was frowning, his hand still reaching for the gun as he watched the blood ooze from her shoulder.

She turned to see who the numbskull that shot her was. In the doorway were two policemen, with Matt at their lead. Matt who was rushing over to her; Matt who was trying to get her to sit down in the armchair, whispering, pleading, "I'm sorry, I'm so so sorry."

From behind her, Brett was asking if she was okay, interspersed with demands to have someone untie him so he could check out her wounds.

Lucille's mind pieced it together. She shoved Matt off her with all the strength in her left arm. "You shot me? You fucking *shot* me? What the fuck?" she bellowed at him.

He kept trying to touch her, apologizing in a steady stream.

"No. Do *not* touch me. I can't believe you fucking shot me!"

Michel appeared at her side. "Are you okay?" He looked concerned, but not overly so, by the sight of his spin doctor bleeding out on his priceless rug.

"No, I am very much not okay! This asshole here shot me!"

"I meant the arm. Does it hurt?" he tried again, his face growing more worried.

"Yes."

"We should get you to a hospital." Now he looked concerned. Maybe it was the close-up of the wound, or maybe Lucille was turning as pale as she felt.

"No shit. First, can you get him away from me?" Lucille had her left arm on Matt's chest, trying to hold him at bay. She needed her strength for the whole not-bleeding-out thing, not tied up dealing with psycho exes.

Michel nodded and put his arm around Matt's shoulder, talking soothingly to him and dragging him away.

She turned to one of the policemen, who were both shifting uneasily in the doorway. "You. Stop standing there, pull out your damn gun, and get this bitch to shut up. I can't hear anything over her whining."

The man shut his mouth and then did as he was told. He held up his gun and pointed it at Sylvia with a steady hand. She fell silent.

Lucille shot a look back at Brett. "Hey, can it. You're not helping either."

"No shit. No one will untie me," Brett growled from his chair.

She wanted to roll her eyes at him but felt that an eye roll would cause her to pass out.

She turned to the other police officer. "Will you untie Mr. Jacobs? Oh, and maybe, I don't know, call an ambulance?"

He hurried to do as he was told.

The room was silent, or close to it. All eyes were on Lucille, waiting for her next move. She wanted to lie down, right there on the rug, and die. It had to be more comfortable than standing here with a bullet wound while a room full of the people she cared the most and the least about in the whole world waited for her to make a decision.

Then, Brett was by her side. He led her over to the armchair and she let him. He pulled his t-shirt off, a little weird and a lot hot, and set to work bandaging up her wounded shoulder as best he could with one arm. He left her side only to retrieve his sling and awkwardly strap it into place across his bare chest and then he was back, crouching beside her and continuing to wrap her injury.

And everyone just watched.

Sometimes inspiring that much fear into people was exhausting.

Lucille sighed and glared at Matt. "Let's start with you."

Brett jogged her arm and she grimaced.

"Sorry," he whispered, and he kissed her skin right above the bullet wound.

"It's okay," she whispered back.

"I really am sorry, Lucy. I had no idea it was you," said Matt, clearing his throat. He'd straightened himself out, stopped muttering apologies, and was now watching Brett like he wanted to tear his head off. *It wouldn't be the first time someone felt that way about Brett*, Lucille almost told him. But stopped. Because he'd shot her. There was an awkward silence as Matt seemed to be waiting for her to accept his apology and she didn't.

"So you normally walk in and shoot the first person you see?" she said instead.

"The first person with a gun cocked who looks ready to fire."

Lucille did roll her eyes this time. "Whatever. How did you even find us?"

If Matt looked contrite before, it was nothing compared to how he looked now. He turned red and stared at the floor.

"You were having me followed, weren't you?"

He didn't respond but gave Lucille her answer in his silence.

"You know what? I'm too furious to deal with this right now. Will you just arrest this woman already?"

"What?" Matt looked confused.

Michel piped in. "And be quiet about it, please. There's been enough commotion in this house for one night. I don't want it known that I was almost murdered in my own home by my former fiancée."

Lucille looked over to Michel with a kind smile. "I was thinking a nice rehab stint for her? You had a domestic dispute because of her drinking problem and the cops were called. She's hurt you one too many times, so you broke it off. Then she goes to rehab, and you're free to do whatever you like."

Michel didn't take his eyes off Sylvia, but he smiled. "You think of everything, Miss Anton."

Matt jumped in. "And again, what?"

Brett finished treating the wound and stood up, topless and unabashed. Matt may have more muscles, but Brett's confident pose right then was far sexier. "Detective, you seem to be off your game here. That's okay, I'll fill you in."

Matt gritted his teeth, glaring at Brett. "I'd rather hear it from Lucille."

"Lucille's a little under the weather at the moment because her dick ex-boyfriend shot her in the shoulder."

Matt actually made a lunge for Brett, catching him off guard and knocking him to the ground. The two police officers pulled their boss off, Sylvia started protesting about her legal rights, and Michel yelled at them all to calm down.

"Hey, hey, cool it," Michel demanded. "What do you say we take this down to the station and get it sorted out there?"

The sound of an ambulance drifted through the air.

"Right on cue," Michel said, grinning like he'd engineered the whole thing out of magic and his own charisma. "Let's get this darling woman to a hospital and, if I'm not mistaken, this guy and the one down-stairs as well. If they aren't dead."

They weren't. Lucille was glad of that. She didn't want her conscience stained with the deaths of two unnamed henchmen. After the drugs started kick-ing in, she was glad of a lot of things. Though not glad Brett wasn't riding with her in the ambulance. Matt had insisted on taking him in one of the squad cars to be questioned. Lucille drifted off from the blood loss and narcotics.

Late in the afternoon the next day, Lucille was re-leased from the hospital. The doctors had removed the bullet, bandaged her shoulder, and stuck the arm in a sling, all in record time. A policeman was stationed outside her door throughout the pro-ceedings. Whether he was there to keep people out or her in wasn't clear but she didn't have any visitors. The hospital was a lonely place to be in without visitors, stuck in a white bed, in a white room, her clarity coming back and her arm throbbing. It gave her too much time to think. If she had a more pos-itive outlook on life, she'd say it gave her a chance to slow down and find the answers to the questions she'd been mulling over. She did not have a positive outlook, but the answers were there regardless. By the time of her release, she felt crappy and spiteful. The negative emotions, however, had less to do with her introspective insight and more to do with her being taken directly to the police station for questioning, thus explaining the speedy treatment.

"What the shit?" she asked from the backseat of the squad car, where she'd been hustled after the nurse wheeled her out to the curb.

"Sorry ma'am, Detective Adams insisted that you be brought to the station as soon as you were able," the policeman replied. He didn't look at her as he spoke, his eyes trained on the road.

At least he knew what was good for him. "Of course he did. Am I being arrested or something?"

Now the man really didn't meet her eyes. "I don't believe so, ma'am. At this point everyone responsible for the incident last night has been brought in."

Lucille scowled and thunked her head against the back of the seat. "Don't call me ma'am."

"Yes..."

At the station, the policeman pulled up to the front and then hurried around to open her door. She didn't have handcuffs on, but he insisted on escorting her through the building to Detective Adams's office.

Lucille scowled again. She'd have preferred handcuffs and an interrogation room with the one-sided glass to whatever intimate conversation awaited her here. With a heavy dose of dread, she entered the office, accepted her orders to sit and wait, and heard the door lock from the outside, trapping her.

The office was a mess. There were papers strewn across the desk, overflowing from open file cabinets, and piled on the floor. In the midst of the clutter was a photo of Matt's family at his sister's graduation from med school, smiling and happy. Another photo sat beside it. A snapshot of her and Matt at the police academy holiday party, young and in love. With her uninjured arm, she swept that one into the overflowing trash can.

The door unlocked and Matt walked in, not looking at her as he made his way around his desk. He dropped more papers on a stack and settled into his office chair. Lucille watched the performance, one eyebrow raised.

He met her eyes. His were tired and sad, his hair unruly from a night of running his hands through it, the gray more prominent. He no longer looked as distinguished and sexy as he had when he'd stormed into Michel's house a few days ago. Now he looked exhausted and desperate, and breaking his heart again would be cruel. Lucille wasn't sure she was still enough of a cold, callous bitch to do that.

"Are you okay?" he asked her, his voice breaking with emotion as he spoke.

She had to be. This was getting pathetic. She had to do this for Matt's own good. If he was ever going to get a girlfriend again, he needed to know there was a zero percent chance it'd be her. "No, I'm not. Some asshole shot me in the arm last night."

Matt ran his hands through his hair. "I said I was sorry about that. Will you— I mean, can you ever forgive me?"

Lucille studied him. "I don't know."

Matt nodded. He looked down at his paperwork and then back at her. "I could have you arrested for breaking and entering Mr. Polce's private residence."

Lucille closed her eyes and shook her head.

He must have misread her reaction because he said, "There's no use denying it. We have you on video." He sounded smug, like he'd caught her.

"Really? That's the tactic you want to go with, Matt? Not the way you get someone to forgive you, especially someone you're clearly pining over."

It was Matt's turn to swallow. "How do you know I'm pining over you?"

"That picture." Lucille pointed to the trash can.

Matt followed her direction to the photo. "Oh. Why is it in the trash?"

In her mind, she went off at him. *Because you, the ex-boyfriend who had my uncle arrested for murder, should not be keeping a photo of me around like some lovesick schmuck!* Out loud she said, "I didn't like how my hair looks."

Matt stared at her for a few minutes, his jaw clenched and his lips pressed together. Then he exploded, "Goddammit, Lucille! God fucking dammit! What is it about you that drives me crazy? You're mean, sarcastic, and frankly kind of a bitch. I am a good guy. I am a good guy and a damn good detective. Yet for some reason, whenever you're around, I become some bumbling idiot who needs your forgiveness so I can get on with my fucking life. One minute I swear to myself I'm over you, and the next you waltz back into my life, all high heels and sarcasm, and lay some grievous offense of mine at my feet. Well, you know what? I'm sick of it. I am sick of these stupid games. I am sick of waiting around for you to realize that I made a mistake eight years ago and that losing you was the worst fucking thing that ever happened to me. I love you. I've always, for some ungodly reason, loved you. Now can we get past all this shit and just be together?"

Matt had been pacing around the room as he talked, gesturing wildly. At the end, he sank to his knees in front of her and grabbed her hand.

The man was persistent to a fault. In some other reality, where they had other jobs and he hadn't shot her or had her uncle arrested, maybe they'd be together. In this reality, he'd given what he probably thought was the most impassioned, romantic speech of his life, a speech in which he'd called her a cruel, sarcastic, heartless bitch. She paused, not because she was at all considering his offer, but in order to decide how best to proceed. Should she let him down gently or just slice off the putrid limb and be done with it?

Whether it was because of the life-changing events of the last few days or not, she didn't have the energy to be cruel. "Matt," she said, removing her hand from his, "I'm sure some day you'll find a woman who will be nice to you and treat you right."

"But you're not that woman?" He looked into her eyes as he talked, his pleading.

"Have I ever been? You said so yourself, I turn you from an intelligent, competent detective into a pleading, bumbling asshole who keeps screwing up and apologizing." She tried to say it kindly, but considering how exhausted she was, it came out biting anyway.

He didn't seem to notice. "You're right. I know you're right." He stood up.

She felt a fleeting sympathy for him. Poor guy. He had terrible taste in women.

Matt smiled and looked back at her. "I was just kidding about still loving you."

Lucille shook her head. "No, you weren't. But that's okay." She stood up and turned to leave.

"I could have your uncle arrested again. After all, he threatened Ms. Walton with an unlicensed gun," Matt said from behind her.

Lucille sighed and turned back to him. "Seriously, Matt. Just stop. Do you really want to have my uncle Simon around here for a few months, possibly years, while you try to get a jury to convict him? Him, here all the time, reminding you of me?"

Matt smiled, but it didn't reach his eyes. "I was joking."

"It was a sad joke." She waited a moment to make sure he was done talking. "I'm going to go now."

Lucille took a few steps. Her hand was on the door handle.

"Are you in love with that idiot Brett?"

She didn't even turn this time, just tilted her head toward him and said, "Whatever helps you sleep at night."

And like that, she opened the door, walked out into the hallway, and was free of Matt Adams for good. She sighed and looked down at her bullet wound. Once this shoulder healed, she could stop thinking about him and cursing his name. Wouldn't that be a relief.

Near the front door of the station she found her uncle, sitting casually on a bench, one leg crossed over the other as he watched police officers milling around.

"Lucy," he said when he saw her, jumping up for a hug.

Her shoulder throbbed. She didn't care. "You did it, didn't you? You got your name cleared?"

He nodded. "Yes. Sylvia's been arrested, Michel's gone home, Beverly has been charged with Cooper's murder. It's all over."

There was a pause as she fought back the tears of relief. It hadn't been an easy couple of days.

"Well, almost over," Simon added.

She pushed back to look at his face. "What do you mean?"

Simon nodded toward the front door. "There's still another of your suitors waiting to talk to you outside."

"If it's Chad my college boyfriend, I am never leaving this building."

Simon laughed. "I've got to hear about Chad sometime. But no, it's just Brett."

"Oh, him? Yeah, I do want to talk to him."

Simon grinned. "I figured you might."

"Shut up."

"What? The guy's growing on me. Plus, he has that tortured artist thing really working for him, and he's best friends with Michel Polce. If you don't talk to him, I will."

Lucille punched him in the arm. "Hey, stop moving in on my man."

"If he's not tied down..." Simon feigned a dash to the door.

Lucille laughed. "I want to hear how you got your charges dropped so quickly."

Simon sighed loudly. "It's actually quite boring and anticlimactic. I'll tell you some time. Now seriously, get out there."

"I will. But there's something I do need to talk to you about first. It's about the business."

# CHAPTER TWENTY-FIVE

Brett was nervous as he waited on the front steps of the police station. Nervous and feeling less than fresh. He was still in the same clothes from the day before. They were the clothes he'd been wearing when he'd had sex with Lucille. The clothes he'd worn to Michel's and then throughout the sweat-producing ordeal of nearly dying and then watching his new maybe-girlfriend nearly die. Then he'd been hauled off to the police station, shirtless under his jacket, interrogated by said maybe-girlfriend's dick of an ex-boyfriend, and had now been waiting outside said station for the last hour, all the while wearing the same clothes. In the rom-com version of this moment, he'd have plenty of time to dash home, shower, change, grab a big bouquet of roses, and catch up with Lucille before she got on her plane to start some exciting job across the country.

In the real-life version, he was terrified of missing her, terrified of leaving this spot in case she walked out through the doors and he never saw her again. Knowing her, she'd change her name and wipe all record of her existence after this. She'd move at once, if she hadn't magically done so while being in the hospital with a gunshot wound. She may be done with this case, but she had other clients and a revolving door of perspectives. Not to mention her fugitive uncle who she'd been reunited with and who treated subterfuge as a lifestyle instead of a necessity.

The uncle who Lucille was now talking to in the station vestibule. Brett could see them in his periphery. His pride told him to look out at the street and pretend to be nonchalant, but his paranoia had him keep one eye on the door at all times.

They'd been standing in that hallway talking for forever. What could they possibly be talking about? Probably him. No, his ego wasn't so inflated as to believe that. Speaking, or rather thinking, of his ego, it didn't feel quite so crippled as before. He didn't have the urge to drink himself into blackness or sex himself numb. He didn't have the urge to write, to have people judge him and criticize him because of the work he'd put out years ago. Was it, could it be possible, he was moving past *The Night Before the Apocalypse*? What did that mean? If he wasn't an alcoholic, failed screenwriter, and the last few days had shown him that he was not, what was he? A whole world of possibilities, the idea of something, anything without his past tempering it, stretched out like a cooling ocean before him. Christ, he was going off the deep end. Here he was, on the steps of a police station, gearing up for some big romantic confession, and he was having an existential crisis.

Still, whatever it was, whatever he did from here on out, it had to be better. He believed it to be better. He already knew what the first step was. If she'd hurry up and get her ass out here.

Lucille left the police station, smiling from her talk with Simon. The sun shone without a cloud in the sky, the city smog beat down on her, and the whole world looked Technicolor.

Brett sat on the steps, his back turned to her, his head angled so she knew he saw her approach. He wore the same clothes from yesterday, now grungy and rough around the edges, his sling showing the worst wear of the ordeal. She didn't look much better. Since everyone had been in police custody while she was hospitalized, no one had brought her clean clothes. Her only option had been Sylvia's blood-stained evening gown. Her hair must have been a sight and her makeup smudged and caked. She'd taken off her heels in Matt's office and couldn't go back to get them now, so she was barefoot under the ruined $56,000 gown. Her shoulder throbbed in its sling. She needed to get her pain prescription filled, but her car was at Michel's house. And first, before any of the hygiene and pain management and practical considerations, she had to find out if Brett would go for the idea she was about to present to him.

Brett stood up as she approached and turned to face her. He looked her up and down, taking in the sling and the dress and her bare feet, and he swallowed, his eyes alight with interest. Lucille exhaled. She thought about saying screw it and making out with him right on these steps. She almost did, and would have, but Brett spoke first.

"Are you okay?"

"Yeah, sort of. It kind of depends," she answered lamely. She was still thinking about fucking him.

Brett nodded. "Things are complicated between you and Detective Adams."

"Uh, no. That's not it."

Brett nodded, and she wasn't sure he believed her.

"Brett. The guy shot me in the shoulder, not to mention tried to send my uncle to jail for a crime he didn't commit, and had me followed. There is no question of that ever working out."

This time Brett smiled when he nodded. "Good. Because...well, I wouldn't like that."

"I know you wouldn't."

Neither of them spoke. The silence was tense and uncomfortable. Lucille decided to bite the bullet and talk first.

"I've been—"

"Did you—?" Brett started saying at the same time.

"You first," Lucille offered.

"No, you. I mean, mine's not that important. Okay, it's kind of important, but maybe it's not? I don't know, but I think it might be. At least to me. About you. Because you are important. To me."

"Honest to God, Brett, just say whatever you're going to say." The man was annoying. Adorable but annoying. Something they were going to have to deal with if this was to work.

"Okay." His next words came out in a rush. "Did you mean what you said when Sylvia was holding us at gunpoint about loving me?"

That was what he was twittering about? "Don't be stupid, of course I didn't mean it. I've only known you for three days. But I do like you." Lucille grinned at him.

"You do?"

"Well, sure."

Brett grinned. "Cool. I mean, I like you too."

As far as romantic speeches went, that was just about perfect. Lucille moved forward until they were on the same level, him a few steps down and her, barefoot, at the top. Brett reached out and pulled her the rest of the way to him with his good arm, gently so as not to hurt her injured shoulder. *What a pair we make*, Lucille thought as he kissed her, gently, sweetly, with all the time in the world.

They kissed for a few minutes or possibly a life-time. Brett pulled back. "What were you going to say?"

"About what?" Lucille was dazed, exhausted, and feeling something like giddiness.

"About whatever you were going to say earlier."

"Right." Lucille nodded. This was the big one. Mu-tual attraction or no, this was the clincher in their relationship. "I'm giving up the business. I talked to my uncle, and he'll be taking over everything. As of about fifteen minutes ago I'm unemployed, and I feel like doing something drastic and rash with my life. Like going straight, becoming an undercover agent for the CIA, and specializing in foreign affairs."

Brett's expression was unreadable. "Okay..."

"That's all you have to say? Okay?" Lucille bit her lip. This was not going well. She took her hand from around Brett's waist and prepared to make a retreat. He didn't let her go.

"Well, yeah, I mean, it's a bit cliché, but you can do whatever you want. It's your life. It's not like you need my permission," Brett said, his grip tightening on her.

He was worried she was leaving him behind. "Don't be a dummy," she said. "I want you to go with me. It's just...I mean, you have your writing career and Michel, and I don't know much about your family but you may not want to leave them..."

Brett's grin was back. He kissed her right in the middle of her speech, an interruption she didn't mind.

"Lucille," he said when he stopped. "Before you walked out here, I was on the verge of an existential crisis about my future. I'm done with the whole alcoholic, failed-screenwriter thing, I don't get along with my family, and I really think it's best for both of us to take some time off from Michel. Something drastic and rash and probably dangerous sounds like exactly what I need in my life right now. Besides it's about time I did something with my PhD in chemistry."

"You have a PhD in chemistry? I had no idea."

"Which is why it's way past time we get to know each other better. Like all the way better," Brett said with a wide grin.

She kissed him. Lucille didn't know when she'd felt so happy, so content, and so unbelievably hungry. This time she pulled back.

"Brett, I'm starving."

He nodded. "Me too. And I need a shower."

Lucille nodded. "But I'm incredibly turned on right now."

"Okay, so food, shower, sex?"

"Sounds divine. But my car is at Michel's."

"So cab to Michel's?"

"Yes, and then food, shower, sex."

"We could always combine the shower and sex," Brett suggested.

Lucille gestured at their injuries. "In our condition? Sex in a bed is going to be tricky. Throw a shower in there and it'll be a mess."

"We could always take a bath."

Lucille kissed him. "I like where this is headed, Mr. Jacobs."

"As do I, Miss Anton."

Brett took her free hand and led her down to the curb to hail a cab.

"Any chance we could throw in picking up our pain med prescriptions in between the cab to Michel's and the food?" Lucille asked as she wrapped her fingers in his.

"You know what? Let's throw caution to the wind and get the pain meds first, then Michel's for your car, food, bath, and sex."

"God, I love you."

"See? Like that. I don't know if you're being serious or if you're just saying that because I'm saying things that you want to hear."

Lucille punched him on the shoulder.

# ACKNOWLEDGEMENTS

If it were not for Ocean's 6, this book would not have been published the first time and certainly would not be getting republished now. Alli, Brittany, Kristin, Leslie, and Scarlett, you have no idea how much your continued support means to me, how much it keeps me writing even then the going feels impossible, and how much I look forward to every one of our chats, retreats, and ad hoc brainstorm sessions.

Thank you to all of my beta readers who have helped me catch plot holes and unintentional character name changes. Thank you to Audrey for editing out my numerous errors and Najla for taking my rambling ideas and turning them into a kickass cover.

And, of course, thank you to my family. Mom and Papa for encouraging me and supporting my writing career from the beginning. Tara and Hannah for listening to my ideas, giving me last minute edits, and for all those summers we spent reading in the parents' living room. Thank you to my fur babies for the cuddles, comfort, and judgmental stares when I'm writing instead of giving them pets.

# **ABOUT**

Celia Mulder, one of the pennames used by author C Mulder, hails from the lovely, yet unpredictable northern Michigan. They are a librarian, a former wedding planner, and an avid appreciator of all things campy and ridiculous. Friends-to-lovers plots are their catnip. They believe in three things-- the importance of representation, the awesomeness of Aquaman, and Buffy the Vampire Slayer. Their first novel Celebrity Spin Doctor was a double RITA award nominee.

# OTHER BOOKS BY CELIA MULDER

**The Celebrity Spin Doctor Series**
Celebrity Spin Doctor
The Issue With Antons
Back On Top

**Novellas**
That Big Romantic Moment
Curses, Quests, and Cuties *in the anthology Magic &*
*Mischief*